What Others Are Saying

"My name is Shayne Lewellyn I bought two of your books at Fort Sill, Oklahoma. I have read the poem and loved the meaning that it sent. I have started to read the first Jo-eb's Quest book, and I can't wait to read more. I read the first few pages, and it was like I was right there. I hope to read more books by you after I finish these."

—Shayne Lewellyn

THE CROOKED TRAIL

THE CROOKED TRAIL

JO-EB'S QUEST

RAYMOND SCHMIDT

TATE PUBLISHING
AND ENTERPRISES, LLC

Jo-Eb's Quest
Copyright © 2015 by Raymond Schmidt. All rights reserved.

No part of this publication may be reproduced, stored in a retrieval system or transmitted in any way by any means, electronic, mechanical, photocopy, recording or otherwise without the prior permission of the author except as provided by USA copyright law.

This novel is a work of fiction. Names, descriptions, entities, and incidents included in the story are products of the author's imagination. Any resemblance to actual persons, events, and entities is entirely coincidental.

The opinions expressed by the author are not necessarily those of Tate Publishing, LLC.

Published by Tate Publishing & Enterprises, LLC
127 E. Trade Center Terrace | Mustang, Oklahoma 73064 USA
1.888.361.9473 | www.tatepublishing.com

Tate Publishing is committed to excellence in the publishing industry. The company reflects the philosophy established by the founders, based on Psalm 68:11,
"The Lord gave the word and great was the company of those who published it."

Book design copyright © 2015 by Tate Publishing, LLC. All rights reserved.
Cover design by Samson Lim
Interior design by Mary Jean Archival

Published in the United States of America

ISBN: 978-1-68142-550-4
Fiction / Action & Adventure
15.10.02

Dedication and recognition is given to those members of my family who have been of a great assistance through direct support, inspiration, and actual contributions to the formation of the details of the story. To my older son, Raymond, for his enthusiastic support; Jon, my younger son for his physical support in rendering directive of content; and to my two grandsons, Raymond and Wesley, for suggestions on how to resolve issues as they arose.

1

Consciousness came about slowly. His first reaction was total confusion and bewilderment. He attempted to open his eyes but was met with a pitch black environment. At first everything was unearthly still. He couldn't make or hear any sounds and was totally disoriented. Dismayed, he felt he was giving in to uncontrollable fear. Then it came to him, a voice was telling him that he had nothing to fear but fear itself. His memory rushed him back to his youth when he was meandering through the old archives, and he latched on to the statement so as to maintain his sanity. "Let's see that was from a man named Winston Churchill, but I don't remember if he was a storyteller or an orator." He could feel the ground shift, and his attention was quickly drawn away from those thoughts as he tried to determine what he was going to do next. "*Body check!*" he exclaimed. "*Shoulders!*" He managed to move some of the muscles in the upper torso. "Arms, hands, and fingers?" He could feel his fingers moving, so he went on, "Legs, ankles, toes." Once again, he managed to ascertain that all the body parts were functioning. Those made him feel better as he now thought that he was regaining some control. Gingerly, he wiped at his eyes in an attempt to wipe away the darkness and hopefully acquire some light. He thought he had his eyes open but couldn't really tell as it was still pitch black. Since he was able to move his hands and eventually his arms, he resolved to roll over and see if anything would present itself. As he turned, he was startled by bright flashes of light like lightning bolts. As they erupted on an irregular basis, he was only able to catch glances and thought he saw some shapes, but he couldn't make them out. Somewhere off in the far distance, he could see a single steady dim-green glow.

"*Where,*" he questioned himself. "*Where am I? What happened, and why is it so dark here?*" He laid there for quite a while, rechecking first his hands, his head, his legs, and then the rest of his body. He wasn't sure exactly where he was or how he'd gotten there. He couldn't remember anything except that somehow he'd come to this place, wherever it was, and was trapped. He scoured his mind once more but came up empty again. "*Okay, let's start with who I am and proceed from there. My name is…*" At that point, everything was blank. He knew that he was a cognoscente being, he was trapped, and the only thing he could do is try to get free. Once again, he looked at the distant green glow and started to inch forward.

Although he wasn't in severe pain, he did feel weak and found it hard to move forward. It seemed that he was in a narrow cave, and he couldn't get up on his knees, as the ceiling was just inches above his head. He would low crawl using his elbows and pushing with the balls of his feet for a while then all but collapse in exhaustion. After a short rest, he would redouble his efforts toward the light, but it seemed the farther he traveled, the dimmer the glow got. At one point, he wondered if he wasn't, in fact, pushing himself backward rather than proceeding forward.

No, that wouldn't make sense, he thought to himself. *My mind is blank for the most part, but I can discern forward from backwards movement. I'll just rest for a minute then go on.* He pulled his elbows back and laid his head on his crossed hands.

This went on for several attempts. He would inch forward, test the walls and the ceiling to see if there was any perceivable difference, and then proceed toward that ever-glowing light. He had no way of knowing how far he had progressed or how far it was to still go. All he knew for sure was that he couldn't stay where he was or he would die. On one occasion, the thought of death crossed his mind. *What was death, what was the opposite of death, and what difference did it make?* While he rested, he contemplated on this issue. *How did he know life from death? How could he know one from the other and how is it that he instinctively knew to go toward that inferno light that never seemed to get any closer?* That much he knew, *but why couldn't he remember anything else?* Once while resting, he searched his mind about these matters and came up blank. He didn't know who he was, why he was here, or even how he came to be here. After a bit, he gave way to exhaustion again, and the darkness overcame him.

He opened his eyes, and the mind started to function again. Something had changed, but he wasn't sure what it was. The passageway seemed to be wider, and when he reached toward the ceiling, he found that he could not touch it. He pushed himself up on his knees and raised his hands once again to see if he could reach the ceiling.

"*Nothing,*" he told himself. "*Nothing but air above.*" With that, he placed one foot on the ground and, supporting himself against the wall, pulled himself up. Soon he was standing, wobbly at first but at last on both feet. "*This has got to be good,*" he said to himself. "*Yes, from this position, I can move quicker, but in which direction?*"

He turned his head to see if he could determine where that light was. It was an eerie feeling because although there was no perceivable source of light, the place where he stood was not completely dark. Rather, it was as if he were in a mist, yet it wasn't wet. Vision was very limited, but at least he could see a couple of feet in front of him. He knew that he'd have to go, but in which way? After contemplating for a few seconds, he decided he'd continue the way he was faced when he woke up. With that, he reached one hand in front of himself while keeping the right hand on the wall. Methodically, he placed one foot in front of the other and observed what happened when he placed his full weight on the forward foot. After several steps, he reckoned that he had mastered the art of traveling like this, but he didn't know just how he knew.

Then as luck would have it, he placed his right foot out to continue to step forward, but there was no solid ground. He yanked the foot back, dropped to his knees, and, with his hand, attempted to determine if there was ground available. Having failed to reach anything, he decided to lie down as close to the edge as he could get and see if he could gather any information by extending his arm as far as he could.

"*Nothing*," he told himself. He raked his hands over the ground and gathered some loose pebbles. He dropped one over the ledge to see if an echo would tell him how deep the crevice was. After he dropped a few, he determined that perhaps the distance to the point of contact was not too far, but when it landed, he heard a splash.

Water, he thought, *or perhaps some other liquid substance.* He took a few more pebbles and tossed them forward to see if he could discern the distance to the other side. After six tries and throwing the pebbles as far as he could, he decided that he couldn't move any farther in this direction, as when the pebbles hit, there was always a splash. What he did know was if he were to lower himself into the liquid, he'd not be able to get back out again, so there was no way he could move forward.

After a minute, he decided to move himself left, away from the wall he'd been using as a guide and see if he could determine a way to get to the left wall. He got upon his knees and began to slowly move toward the distant wall. As he did, something strange seemed to be happening. He knew he was moving away from the right wall, but the farther he moved in that direction, the distance from the right wall didn't become greater.

My mind must be playing tricks on me, he thought. *I know I'm moving, yet the wall at my back never seems to be any farther away. The wall must be moving.* He continued this cat-and-mouse game for the better part of a half hour then stopped. Once again, he reached behind him only to find that the wall was still directly behind. He took a few pebbles from his pouch and tossed them in the direction of the abyss where the lake had been. To his surprise, the report indicated that he was no longer throwing into a liquid.

"*Okay,*" he said to himself. "*If I can now continue to go forward, that is what I'll do.*" He lowered himself to his knees and turned back to the original course.

With a mechanical, deliberate motion, he placed his hands forward and did a cursory sweep of the area. In that fashion, he continued to move forward. Once he convinced himself that it was safe and his confidence returned, he stood up.

He became aware that the light in the cave had become brighter, and he was able to see several feet in front of him. "*This is good,*" he said to himself. "*This is real good.*" Just as he was telling himself that things were better, the ground beneath him gave way, and he slipped down a slide toward the bottom. "*This is bad, this is real bad"* was his immediate reaction.

The drop was angled, so it was not a real fall; it was more like tumbling down the side of a hill. He reached out, but there was nothing to grab onto. He scooped a handful of gravel as continued his journey downward. When he reached what he perceived to be the bottom he recycled his thought pattern and started taking stock of himself. *Nothing broken!* he thought to himself. *My thick clothing saved me from being cut by the rocks while I fell, and except for my dignity being hurt, I only suffered a few bruises on my neck and forehead.* Exhaustion had taken its toll, he slumped to rest for a minute and he slipped back into the darkness.

When he came to, he determined that things were different. For one thing, he was no longer in an environment where light came from nowhere and visibility was limited. He was in a large room, lying on a bed of straw, and the light source was torches. He moved his head first to one side then the other. As his vision cleared, he could see movement off to the far side of the room and hear what seemed to be a conversation going on. He couldn't understand what was being said, but whatever it was, it was surely about him, and it seemed that there were two sides to the conversation. He decided to sit up and see if he could ask any questions. As he attempted to rise, he determined quickly that he was securely tied, and except for his ability to move his head, his movement was severely restricted. He determined that he would just listen to the commotion at the far side of the room and wait. After what seemed to be an eternity, he decided to see if he could communicate with them.

"Forgive me," he started. "Can anyone tell me where I am or how I got here?"

The conversation stopped abruptly, and it seemed that a dozen pairs of eyes were staring at him. Nothing was said, and no one moved. It was almost as if they were petrified.

Looking determined not to be a guinea pig, he continued, "I don't know who you are or why you have tied me down, but I am a human being and am entitled to be treated as such."

After a minute, one of the pair of eyes came toward him. He could make out that this person was obviously one of intellect and was the same as him yet different.

The person was dressed in a long flowing garb that seemed to consist of blue and red streamers. As the person approached him, he heard a voice that seemed to be a female saying something he didn't understand. Although he couldn't understand the words, he felt deep inside that the emotions being displayed showed compassion and was caring toward him. With a show of what could only be described as compassion she reached out and touched his forehead. In some sort of broken English and some other language he'd never heard before, she simply asked him to stay quiet for a while. He took reassurance with that and decided that since he had no alternative anyway, he'd abide by her request. So once again, he simply looked toward the direction where the conversation was coming from.

He'd listen intently for a while, trying to determine if he could pick out any words that he might recognize, and as the conversation droned on, he'd lapse in and out of a seminoma. The next time he opened his eyes, he felt his forehead being wiped with a damp cloth. The same person was attending to him that had approached him the first time.

She started, "We have determined that you are not a wild animal and, as such, are an intelligent being. So…" She hesitated for a few seconds. "We've decided not to kill you right away. This world is made up of both good and bad people, and before your fate is determined, I have convinced them that we need to be sure that you are not a threat."

"Thank you!" he responded, His tone gave away his emotions, a combination of fear and disgust as she immediately recoiled.

"It would be safer for us if we simply killed you right now and dropped your body into the well of fire."

"But?" he inquired. "What good would that do to you or your people? You might be squandering a valuable resource." As he spoke he continued to test his ability to move and found that he was securely bound.

"Perhaps," was the reply. "But safety is of paramount in our society, and with that, progress has been very slow."

"Well," he continued, "is it possible to get something to eat? I don't know how long I've been without food, and I know I'll need to take in sustenance or I'll perish."

She moved a bowl of soup closer to him and started to spoon-feed him. His first taste surprised him, as it had a slight sweet taste to it.

"It's what we feed our very young," she said. "Once you've regained some strength, you'll be able to eat more solid food." She paused for a second and stated, "If you are allowed to live that long." Her voice resonated a sense of hope and doom. "Since we've determined that you are a cognizant creature, I have convinced them to hold off on an execution until we can determine if you are a threat to our civilization or not."

"I am here not of my own accord," he started. "I have been placed into this situation by an accident. The earth where I came from caved in on me, and my only way to attempt to save myself was to proceed toward a green glow in the far-off distance. I don't know how long I followed that light or how many times I succumbed to unconsciousness. Right now, all I know is that I am still alive, and for some reason, God has spared my life."

"God!" was the reply. Her eyes widened, and her lips quivered. She suddenly turned and hurried away. He was left wondering just what he had said that threw her into a panic. Surely, they knew of God. After all, they could recognize intelligence, and the room showed signs of intelligent design. There were tables, chairs, beds, mirrors, and designs that hung on the wall. There was no doubt that they were an intelligent race. Yet something kept nagging in the back of his mind. *What was it that was different with these people? How was it that they knew of the existence of other humans yet had such fear of making contact?* As his movements were severely restricted, he had nothing but his mind to make work, so he attempted to concentrate on what he knew.

Later—he didn't know how long, as he had drifted in and out of consciousness several times—he was approached by yet another being. This time, it was a man in long dark robes with a crown on his head.

"You spoke of a God. How is it that you dare to mention him in the presence of my people?"

Jo-Eb decided to grab the initiative and responded, "Your people? Why do you call them your people? Are they not intelligent individuals who can make up their own minds about the existence of God?"

"Enough!" came a harsh, commanding reply. "You will not mention this God again." With that, he simply turned and started to walk out.

"Enough," Jo-Eb responded. "It's not nearly enough. You control by fear and not logic. You do not even know the God of which I speak. You will only control them for a short while, then you yourself will answer to the Almighty God." He felt his chest rising as his anger flourished. "Are you such a coward that you cannot face truth? Has the seeking of security outweighed your senses? Do you walk in the darkness because you fear the light?"

The man stopped in his tracks. "You don't understand, and it's not my job or intent to attempt to explain it to you. I'll take this up with the council, and your fate will rest in their hands."

"You do just that, and I will rely on my God to determine my fate. If He ends it here and now, then I will die knowing that I have served him faithfully."

The man swung his arm around in a wide arc, his robe following like a sail in the wind, and he quickly departed. After a bit, he heard a voice from behind the curtain: "You didn't make any friends there." The voice was of the female again and was almost whimsical.

"I have heard of your God over the ages but never thought I'd meet anyone who would actually buck up to him. He is the high priest of the tabernacle and a very powerful man."

"He's a schmuck," Jo-Eb responded. "He's arrogant, self-righteous, pompous, and wrong." With that, he allowed himself a slight smile. He might be going to his death without ever knowing who he was, but he was confident that he had made the correct decision.

He had no way of knowing how long it was, as there had been no morning, no high noon, or an evening with the stars out. All he knew was he remained tied to the bed for a long time. Once in a while, he was untied long enough to go to the privy and relieve himself. When this opportunity arose, he made sure to exercise himself as best and as long as he could get away with it. He got to know his guards, and although they were not aggressive toward him, they let it be known that in no uncertain terms, he would meet harsh punishment if he were to attempt to escape.

Escape. That was a thought, but which way would he go? He didn't know anything about what the rest of their world was like and wouldn't know which way to go if he did attain a certain amount of freedom. His instinct would be to climb as his last vestige of consciousness had indicated that he was falling into a deep hole. He decided to put that out of his mind and concentrate on how he could find out more about this civilization.

For instance, he did not understand anything about the makeup of their language. Even those who seemed to show some compassion for him could not converse with him, as they didn't understand any language that he had any command of. So he resolved to attempt to learn their language by possessive nouns. He would point to an item and repeat the word in English with a question mark at the end of each statement. After a while, he was able to discern some of the words.

On one occasion, he was pointing to himself and initiated the word *human*. The guard laughed at him and then pointed to himself and stated emphatically, "Human." Then he pointed to Jo-Eb and spoke, "你是未知." Since he had no way of identifying what had been said, he simply kept it for a later time and resolved to ask the female in change of him if she could translate it for him.

"You are the unknown," she responded. "We are humans, but you are an obvious mutant."

He didn't know what to make of that, so he inquired, "How do you interpret it that I am a mutant?"

"Just look at yourself," she replied. "You only have two eyes and not one on either side of your head. You only have two arms instead of four, and you are much taller than we are. It's obvious that you are a throwback or a mutant that failed to evolve into a full human."

He was taken aback with that response and decided he'd not say more about it until his memory would return. During all this, he still didn't know who he was, where he came from or—other than his belief in God—what he was doing here or how he even got here.

He learned that according to their culture, the lights were dimmed and relighted once a day. As far as he could make out, this happened at approximately the same time each cycle. As close as he could figure it, it closely responded to twelve-hour increments. He formulated that it was as significant to them so as to mark what would be a daily routine. Eventually, bars were constructed around his room, and he was allowed to move about in his cell. His conclusion was that they—for whatever reason—had elected not to kill him, at least not right away. With that in mind, he requested to be afforded any written script that might be available. The curators simply laughed at him and responded, "Since you don't know the language, how do you expect to read any of it?" While this was true, he determined that it wouldn't stop him from making inquiries. He asked if anyone would teach him the language. Again, laughter resonated throughout the halls.

After the laughter died down, a young boy entered the cell room. He was rather shy and very reserved, but nonetheless, he introduced himself. 我叫保罗"[My name is Paul] he started. "保罗, 你是谁?[Paul, who are you]"As he pointed to Jo-Eb.

The only thing Jo-Eb could distinguish was that the statement started when the young man pointed to himself and ended with a question as he pointed to Jo-Eb. He repeated the first part 保罗 [Paul] as he pointed to the boy and 你是谁？[who are you] as he pointed to himself. The boy simply shook his head in wonder. Jo-Eb knew that he was being asked for his name, but he didn't know it. So he decided to pick up objects and repeat them in English, thus allowing the boy to repeat them in his own language. This established a routine whereby the boy would arrive at a specific time, teach him the language one step at a time, and then leave. When he returned, he would test Jo-Eb to determine how much he had retained. After what was akin to several meetings, perhaps two weeks in worldly time, he tested Jo-Eb on several subjects to determine how well he was doing. The woman would come back from time to time, and that was when he was able to ask questions in English. As time went on, she was using less and less English and demanding that he speak only in her language.

The subject of God did not come up again, so he asked on one occasion about their cultural beliefs and their worship routine. He had determined that they did have a routine where they spent some time in what he would refer to as prayer. He made sure not to mention God by name but asked for information that would seem nonthreatening. When he was asked why he wanted this information, he responded that if he was to understand the culture and not just the physical world, he would have to learn as much about their way of life as he could. This seemed to satisfy his young trainer, Paul, who seemed to accept his inquiries as interest and progressive and not aggressive in nature.

One day, Paul brought in a young woman with him. He introduced her as a friend and indicated that he would leave them alone for a while so they could get to know each other better. After he left, she advanced toward Jo-Eb to seduce him. He immediately recoiled at the thought. In all his years, he had never simply allowed himself to engage in this type of behavior on a whim—not that he was not able, but he thought that it was his upbringing and an installed respect for women that he would not compromise himself. She attempted on a couple more occasions to present herself, and he simply refused. After a bit, Paul returned and spoke with the young woman. "She says that you refused her. Perhaps because she is ugly by your standards?"

"No," Jo-Eb replied, "it's not that. The truth is I find her very attractive. However, in the world where I was raised, it is not proper for a couple to engage in such activities without being committed to each other for life."

"What a strange practice," was the reply. "I thought you'd enjoy some female company. That's why I brought her in."

"Oh," Jo-Eb responded, "it's not that I don't enjoy female company. It's just that those specific acts are considered degrading to the woman unless it is a mutual understanding that a lifetime commitment is involved."

"You mean nobody does it unless they are linked for their entire life?"

"Just as your civilization has rules and protocol to follow and you have those who do not follow it all the time, we also have those who do not follow what we know in our hearts to be right."

"So be it!" Paul replied. "I'll not place you in that situation again. If it is to be, then the natural order of things will prevail. Actually, I'm glad to have you inform me of this, as it has always been my contention that you are not an animal but that you live by a certain standard and your actions have proved me to be right."

As time passed, Jo-Eb became more adept in the language, and a certain trust was established. As such, he was allowed—at first accompanied by guards—to wonder about the area without teeters. Although he was required to wear an armband with bright red and yellow stripes. He hardly thought that necessary as he only had two eyes and two arms and could readily be identified without an arm band, but nevertheless, he followed the dictates of his captors. In all the time he spent in that area, he never felt a free man. Eventually, he was assigned task to perform as they explained that every member of the community, no matter how great or small, was required to contribute to the community. As he gained more and more latitude and was able to converse with the locals, he managed to strike up several conversations. In this world, there were those who welcomed his presence and his inquiries, as they were also curious about the place where he came from. For a long time, he wasn't able to provide much information. Then one day, he discovered that the things that he had been learning here seemed to relate to those types of things that would relate to his world, and he found bits and pieces of his memory were returning.

One day as he was wandering through the residential area, he spotted a building that reminded him of a place and a time so long ago. At first, he didn't know what it was all about, but as he contemplated on it, the puzzle pieces came to light. This edifice was almost an exact duplicate of the structure that he and Olivia had planned before it was burned to the ground. With that, a flood of memories returned. Suddenly, he knew his name, where he came from, and that he indeed had a wife and several children somewhere. At first, he experienced elation then depression at the thought that he'd been gone so long and had no way of knowing what had happened to his family. As he gave further thought to it, his memory of Jana and his unborn son came into view. He couldn't help himself; he simply sat and wept profusely. One young girl came up to him and inquired if she could be of service, to which he replied, "Thank you, but my pain is not external but internal."

"We all have our bad times," she replied.

As he looked up, he saw that she also wore the bright red and yellow band on her arm and that she too had only two eyes and two arms. *How could this be?* he thought to himself. He thought that he was the only outcast in this civilization.

"Oh," she exclaimed, "I was found as an infant and raised by my parents. My name is Tabatha. They are very loving and have accepted me not as a freak as many do but as an individual who has a right standing with God."

He couldn't believe his eyes and ears. Someone actually said the word *God* and did not recoil at the thought. "What do you know of this God?" he inquired. "How is it that you are not afraid to mention it when so many others recoil at the very mention of the word?"

She looked at him quizzically for a minute then responded, "Oh, have you not been informed that there are, in fact, two divisions in our land. The people who first found you are believers in a god of war and turmoil, 卧云宇 (Guan Yu), and we, on the other hand, have determined that the God of the world from which I came holds the truth of life. You see, when I was found, I was accompanied by script that we refer to as the Bible. My parents, at first, thought to burn it as being heretical then decided that perhaps it could open some doors to provide insight as to what I am. As they read the books, they taught them to me, and I, as I was raised among the other children, would discuss these matters with them. As they read from the books of this strange bible, they decided to teach them to me. I as a person from a different world was allowed to be raised with the other children in the hope that they could steer me in the right direction. As I discussed these matters with them, many came to believe as I do. Now there is actually quite a following of the Word of God and an acceptance of Jesus Christ as the Savior of our world."

Jo-Eb was filled with joy that he had met someone else that believed as he did but was dubious as to having discussions with Paul and the others of that sector, as he could feel the animosity within their hearts. That being the case, he always managed to tame his tongue when in their company.

One day, Paul asked where he traveled off to so often. He told them of the girl and the residential area where he had met her. He didn't mention that she and her compatriots had a belief in God as he did. Paul invited himself along, and Jo-Eb gladly accepted. He thought perhaps in his wildest dreams that Paul would somehow be exposed to the truth and to accept it. That was his hope anyway. When they arrived, he introduced Paul to a young group of mainly women and noticed that Paul took an immediate shine to the one called Moranda. He and Tabatha introduced the members to Paul, and he, in turn, introduced himself as a member of the protectorates. Although they said nothing, Jo-Eb could feel the tension arise. Many of those gathered simply had other things to do at this time and excused themselves. Moranda seemed to take a liking to Paul and decided that her chores could wait. So they spent the afternoon exchanging stories of their dreams and aspirations.

"One day, I hope to be able to return to my original world to see if it is actually as bright as the stories that I've heard," Tabatha said this as if nobody was listening.

"You'll only find hatred and heartache there," Paul responded. "We have documents from that world that have been passed down through the centuries that reveal the true nature of that world. Although…" He reflected for a moment. "I must admit that we've found something in Jo-Eb that we did not expect to find. We found out that amongst all the turmoil up there that there is cause for hope that one day we could go there and conquer that world for the benefit of the civilization. Actually, that is why Jo-Eb wasn't killed immediately, as there are those among us that desire to find out as much as possible to enable that very thing to happen."

Jo-Eb looked him in a way that he had never thought of before. He had always thought of Paul as a friend even under these strange circumstances.

"Oh, don't look at me like that," Paul stated with a slight grin on his face. "I have never contemplated having you killed or to expose you to torcher in order to gain information on your world. That is for the politicians and the war mongrels to do. I am of the house of the protectorates and closely guard our way of life, but I am not an ogress. I believe that it is best to live and let live."

Jo-Eb felt somewhat better about that, but something told him not to drop his guard.

He met on several more occasions and met Tabatha's parents. Once they were comfortable with him and determined that he was not a threat to their daughter or their way of life, they invited him into their home for dinners and other social occasions. For some reason, Paul never returned with him, but he was informed that Paul had been meeting Moranda on occasion, and they seemed to be hitting it off quite well. Despite this obvious relationship formulating between them, Jo-Eb found that he was advising Tabatha to be careful when around Moranda, as he was uneasy with the two of them, and from the questions Paul had been asking, he felt uneasy about the situation. Tabatha mentioned it to Moranda who sluffed it off as an obviously overcautious mind.

As it turned out, Tabatha's father, 旅行者 (the traveler), was an explorer of some renown. He had traveled extensively throughout the land, and although not a member of the protectorate, he had brought many valuable objects back to the head of that family and presented many of them as gifts. This had placed him in a special category of acceptable although he was not formally a member of the clan. He had explored many heretofore undiscovered caves. Jo-Eb enthusiastically accepted the invitation for him to join an expedition when the subject was approached. But first, he would have to get permission from the protectorates, as he never lost sight of the fact that he was their property. The discussion wasn't long or particularly eventful. He was informed that he was allowed to accompany the traveler, but that he was to make a full report upon completion of each expedition. He readily agreed and, as such, was given permission to accompany him on his outings.

They went on a few outings not too far from home, and Jo-Eb gained the confidence of the traveler, as he had quite a bit of knowledge that he had learned from Albert about rock formations and consistency of the makeup of the land. On his last trip, he stayed overnight at the traveler's home so as to get an early start the next day. He wasn't sure exactly what was being planned, but he knew from the excitement that something unusual was going to happen. They arose very early that morning, and he found that not only the three that usually accompanied him on his trips were present but that there were several people dressed and readied for the occasion. There were many women and children in the group, and they were very quiet.

They traveled quickly and quietly along the path. He noticed that as they proceeded, others came from out of the hills and joined his band. They traveled for almost three days with little or no rest. At this point, Tabatha's father approached him. "Jo-Eb," he stated, "we are the outcast of the society in which we live. We have given ourselves to the God of your Bible and profess belief in the Jesus of that script. That very fact has caused us to be outcast, and many have been persecuted because of it. I had always been seeking for a way to lead my people out of this oppression but until you came along, I didn't know how. Now I've been given an insight as to how that will happen. Through your knowledge of the exterior world and our desire to be free of the chains of the ruling clan, we have decided to leave our homes and seek a new life above. By the time we reach our destination, we will have some three hundred soldiers and a multitude of families. I couldn't tell you this earlier for fear of you letting it slip."

Jo-Eb didn't know if he should be flattered or angry that this had all happened right under his nose. When he put it all together, it made sense. Tabatha had befriended him, and her father and friends accepted him without reservation. Being thankful that he had been accepted into a community, he had placed himself in a position to go along with and indeed lead this group out of their offensive lives. They took stock of their bearings and belongings and continued on toward the area where the traveler had directed them to go.

After two more days of travel, they entered a huge cave that seemed like it could house thousands of people. He found that some were already present and was told that the last contingency would arrive on the morrow. At that time, they would enter the bowls of the cave, and there would be a hard, long climb up the successive levels. It all had been planned well, as they found plenty of food, water, and other materials required for the climb. Litters had been erected for those too weak to climb on their own, and several stop points had been established.

"We've been planning this for a long time, and I've actually been to the top twice and exited the cave. The land beyond seems to be hilly and filled with green grass and trees. That will be strange to the majority of them, as most have only read about things such as trees in the Old Testament of the Scriptures. I have been informed that the last group has arrived, and we must start our climb immediately. Someone has been following us and has reported to the protectorate that we are attempting to leave. They, of course, have no intention of letting us go and will kill all who oppose them. If they catch us, it will be an ungodly slaughter."

With that, he started the first elements of the climbers. Jo-Eb and a few others remained to ensure that all the travelers were accounted for and had started on the journey. He could see the fear in the eyes of those toward the rear of the column and mentioned to the traveler that he noted the formation of the rocks at the cave entrance. He stated that once the last of the final group had reached a point at the bend of the cave, he could ignite an explosion that would cause the mouth of the cave to collapse. It entailed a certain risk, but he was confident that if he could pull it off, it would slow the opposition down to preclude them from following.

"Just like the parting of the Red Sea," the traveler exclaimed. "Only instead of drowning the pursuers, they will be blocked from the entrance and have to return to their own lands. I am happy that this can be, as I left several friends behind who did not believe as we do but were not actively opposed to us. They would, of course, be included in the army of pursuers, as they are obligated to do so under current law."

They climbed for seven days, and after the final group left a rest stop, it was destroyed so as to cause any of them intent on following them the hardship of sustaining the pursuit. The hope was that eventually the aggressors would simply give up. The traveler had hoped to be able to leave the cave open so that he could return some day and selectively offer freedom to any whom he thought might be interested. What they found though was that despite their best efforts, the enemy continued their pursuit. They were several levels below but garnered no intent to quit. That being the case, he gave the final order to collapse the final exit. Tons of rock and debris plummeted toward the bottom. He really regretted having to give that order, as he knew some of those who would be killed were conscripts and friends.

They spent several weeks getting adjusted to the new environment. Some experienced cold like they never knew existed. The brightness of the sun was a problem to many of them, and they found that the vegetation was sparse with only a few trees about. Jo-Eb suggested that they camp in an area where there seemed to be some water and some shelter from the extreme cold and the blistering heat of the day. He recognized this area as a desert area with a rather large oasis that would sustain them for a while. After he attained his bearings, he decided to search west to see if he could determine exactly where they were. As luck would have it after only one day of travel, he came to the edge of a cliff. On the other side, he could see an abundance of trees and what seemed to be vegetation. He was convinced that this could be a starting point for the new community.

When the traveler saw the spot, he was very happy. The cliffs were steep and deep but not impassable. After all they had been through, he was sure they could reach that area in short order and establish a new community. Although it really wasn't necessary, Jo-Eb felt he had to explain to them that since they were now in a new world, as he put it, they would find many things strange to their way of thinking. For one thing, all the humans he'd ever run into had only two eyes and two arms. It seemed to dismay some of them, as they held no animosity toward those like him.

"You will find many good people who will accept you as you are, and just like in the land where you came from, you will encounter those who are narrow-minded and afraid of the physical differences. I am sure with the traveler's guidance, you will be able to establish your community. I just wanted to caution you that there are both good and not-so-good people in this world. Don't give way to the temptation that will undoubtedly enter your minds that all of these people are bad." He spent several more weeks with them, and once he was confident that they were a flourishing community, he told the traveler and his family he had to go on with the mission that he had been sidetracked away from so long ago.

He determined to continue his way west to the great divide and make his way back to his home and Olivia. He wondered what had happened to her. He had been gone a long time and with no word except that perhaps he'd been killed in the earthquake. He didn't know what to expect.

2

He managed to reach the divide in a relatively short period. As he came out of the forest, he spotted the fortress that he had come upon so many years ago. It seemed bigger now, and he noted that there were even some log cabins outside the fort. The stream of water that he had once dipped his kerchief into to wipe his forehead was larger now, and he could see improvements that indicated that they had damned the river and could better control the flow. He smiled as he, once again, entered the main gate and passed a guard standing there without movement and sporting a huge sword. He wondered for a minute if it was the same guard when the man simply said, "Welcome back."

He proceeded to the blacksmith area where the smithy met him and presented him with a coin. "You had this coming since I didn't get to finish it the last time. Things are different now. We're actually considered a township. For one, I'm happy you got rid of that witch."

"Thanks," Jo-Eb replied, "but you can keep the coin, and if you will do some repairs on this one, I'll make up the difference." He pulled the sword from the scabbard and presented it to the smithy.

"Well," he replied, "this one isn't banged up as nearly as bad as the other. I'll do it for the one coin."

Jo-Eb motioned that he was going to go to the dining hall and get some grub.

"You'll find us a lot friendlier this time. Whatever happened to the old man?"

Jo-Eb took a minute to outline their travel together and wound up with, "I'm hoping to see him again soon." With that, he went toward the dining hall.

Jo-Eb stayed there for two more nights as he gathered grub and other articles he expected that he'd need for the trip. He listened to the stories of those both heading east and west and determined that this indeed was a place that would thrive and become a waypoint for future generations. On the morning of the third day, he arose early, retrieved his gear, and once again headed west.

The road this time was more populous and friendlier, and he was able to cover a lot of land in a very short order.

In just a few weeks, he was standing on the hill where he had last seen Olivia and the children. He was apprehensive since it had been a long time and he had no way of knowing what had transpired in his absence.

He could see the olive grove in the valley, and his chest began to pump faster as he anticipated how he would be received once again. As he entered the town, he noticed that several things had changed. The two towns had grown closer, and he vaguely recognized a few of the folks. When he arrived at Olivia's father's house, he was greeted with a mixture of joy and sorrow. It seemed that when she had received the notice that he had died, she was determined to go to find out if his body could be retrieved so he could have a proper burial. She had taken the entire family and headed east to see if she could recover his body and bring him home. That was well over two years ago, and she had not been heard from since. That left him with no other choice except to retrace his steps to attempt to locate her once again.

It seemed that now he was on another quest. "Is it never going to end?" he questioned himself. "Will my travels never come to a conclusion?" He just shook his head, said his good-byes, and once again headed east. His plan was to get back with Olivia and the children and return to their home. He thought that as all that had happened and the length of time that had passed when he first went looking for Flower, he'd just discontinue the search. "After all," he reckoned, "Aunt Martha had passed some time ago," and he really didn't think that the rest of the clan would have other than a passing interest in what had transpired over the past several years. It was time, he determined, to settle down and make the life that he and Olivia had planned so long ago. He traveled the route as he remembered it and found, not to his surprise, new settlements cropping up as he journeyed. As he was able to establish that he was known by some in these parts he found, folks received him without anticipation. It seemed the entire region was now flourishing.

Since he had managed such good time and it would only be a day out of the way, he determined to pass by Abraham's place and see how that clan was coming along. He was sure that Abraham and Melissa would have it well in tow, yet he wanted to see for himself. Also, he was really interested in how young Jo-Eb had come out. He kept telling himself that, but the real reason was he wanted to once again visit the grave of his first love. He never got over that even with Olivia as a soul mate. He just couldn't shake the thought that one day he'd once again sit with her. Sometimes he'd wonder how it will all work out since he now had two loves that he had an allegiance with. "I'll just have to let God work that out," he told himself. So for a short while, he veered from his path and headed for a land that he had come to love. It seemed like another world and another time, yet he couldn't shake the feeling nor did he want to.

The visit was short as he expected it to be. Melissa was expecting again, and they already had eight. The triplets had been born a year ago, but young Jo-Eb and his younger sister were there to help run the house when their dad was away on a trip. He didn't return while Jo-Eb was there, but young Jo-Eb promised that he'd let his dad know and was sure he'd be pleased that he wasn't, in fact, dead as reported.

That next morning, he visited Jana's' grave site once again and prayed a prayer of sorrow and thankfulness that she was at rest in God's arms forever. He tarried there for over two hours, hoping to see the bird again with the olive branch, but it did not appear. Finally, he spoke once again with the sorrow mixed with the joy of knowing that his Jana and their baby were, in fact, happy with God. At last, he got up and headed back on his quest to find Olivia and the children. As he traveled, he reflected on the passage of time and the new life that he had been given. He knew that he'd never be at peace with himself if he allowed grief and anger to rule him. With that, he determined that although he would indeed always remember Jana, he would accept the life that he had been given and strive to do the will of God.

He proceeded with haste toward his destination, wondering just what he would find upon his arrival. For the next several days, he traveled quickly for long periods and stopped to sleep only when necessary. Finally, he arrived at what used to be the forbidden land where the closed society had caused him to go many days out of his way in order to respect their boundaries. This time, however, as he approached the once-forbidden land, he found it to be a new environment. He was met by a small group of guards who, although they didn't know him personally, had heard of his story and how he'd been lost in the great quake that devastated much of the land. That event was some two years in the past now, and a lot had happened since then. New routes were opened, the barbaric tribes from the north had been driven back, and commerce once again had taken root.

As he approached the city, he noticed that a new complex of buildings had gone up, and although much of the old architecture still remained, a scene of the new culture was taken root within. He met many of his old adversaries and was thrilled to hear that Olivia and her children had passed through this way on her way to the green land. Messengers were dispatched immediately to announce the good news of his return. As night was falling, he opted to accept their hospitality and figured he'd proceed the next day. This was a mixed sorrowful and joyful event, as he learned that some of his fellow compatriots had been killed in the battles with the northern tribes, yet the joy outshined the pain of their loss when the wives and their children gathered around him and proclaimed that it was because of him that even with their loss, life would carry on, and they were thankful for his presence. The evening festivities went well into the night, but at last, he reluctantly retired.

On the morrow, he once again set out to find his family. He wasn't sure just what he'd say to Olivia and the kids. He wanted it to be a happy time, and he now wanted to at last settle down and to provide the life for his family that he had always wanted. After a couple of days, he once again spotted the building where he and Albert had first established their outpost. It was quite a bit larger now and showed signs of a small, thriving community. He couldn't verbalize the joy he felt as he proceeded forward in anticipation of their reunion. His arrival caused quite a stir, as friends greeted him with joy and beaming support stories. Albert had married and now had two very young ones and the land that was once-barren rock sprouted an organized farmland of luscious green vegetables.

    He was ecstatic to see all of them, but the question pertaining to his family still persisted. No one could tell exactly what had happened to them. The last anyone had heard, Olivia and the children were heading farther east past the great divide in an attempt to reunite with his family back in Kentucky. Although she didn't know any of them, she felt it was her obligation to reunite with his family. They had been gone for quite some time now, and there was no news coming from that direction, so they did not know what to expect. Jo-Eb determined that once again he must move on in the hope of catching and reuniting with the family. Now what had started so long ago as a simple quest found him facing new challenges to an ever-lengthening road.

3

He leaned slightly forward, his elbow on his right knee and his hand stroking his long red beard. He sat for the longest time then, in a tone somewhat testy, said, "It seems we have a situation here where hawks and doves are at odds again. You, Jagaren, the head of the Thunderbolt clan, want to behead the fellow on the spot. Since you are known as the Hungarian Destroyer focused on conquest without mercy, I'd say your mother must have had a vision of your character while you, Chun Leargas, were aptly named as one who enlightens and have become the leader of the dovish Halcyon clan, desire leniency. Your mother always said you had the smiling eyes of the Irish." The emphasis on dovish left no doubt the king was leaning toward the hawks' desires. "Your differences are complex, and your firm stance in your desire to present your case makes things difficult and bothersome. You, Jagaren, state he is a bother and we should dispatch him quickly, get it over, and be done. On the other hand, Chun Leargas presents the case in terms of civility and compassion. You want to spare him and attempt to rehabilitate him. Your position that it's a God-given right for a human to be treated with respect and life is precious and has merit, but it's costly. Human rights have been a contentious subject for generations, and whatever decision I make today won't change that."

He slid to the back of the chair, wiped his face with both hands, stretched his arms, and then placed his hands behind his head as he looked toward the ceiling. It seemed like forever since he had been able to just sit back, contemplate on the cracks on the wall, and rest. The battle with the Harmonies had lasted several weeks, and he had very little rest, let alone sleep. Finally, he said, "Place him in chains. Be sure to feed him." He said as an afterthought, "I'm taking a long rest, and we'll get back to this in the morning."

As a young lad, he had often contemplated on the glory of battle and the thought that he'd be the king of the capital city and seat of the empire. It was a territory that spanned as far west to the Rockies and to the east as far as the wide water known as the little divide. His father was a glorious warrior and managed to spread the influence of the SW empire all the way to the cold lands in the north to the southern border where a great canal was said to once present a connection of the two oceans. Sometimes he thought he'd like to kick his old man in the pants for being so aggressive. He loved his father and mourned his death after a battle in a faraway province in some little village he didn't even know the name of, but nonetheless, he was left with the responsibility to govern it. He lay there for a long while, wondering if he was ever going to sleep again. He couldn't get that fellow out of his mind. At long last, he drifted off, as sheer exhaustion took its toll.

The next morning, it seemed to be different. They had let him sleep long into the morning, and he felt refreshed. The first order of business though, even before breakfast, was brought before him. It was the thought that he had to make a decision on the prisoner, and that served to ruin his day. The prisoner was still there, and he alone had to decide his fate. He called for his attendants and was in the process of ordering his food when the guards brought the man in. He looked like he'd been beaten and battered. His clothing was torn and bloody, and he stumbled as the guard pushed him to his knees with a harsh, "Down on your knees, scum."

King Roger raised his hand and waived the guard off. He was used to seeing wretches kicked and beaten, but in this case, it seemed harsh to do it just out of spite and anger. "Got anger problems?" He directed his comments to the guard. "How is it you treat a person harshly before you know if he's to be a guest or a prisoner?"

The man struggled to get up, and the king motioned to the guard to assist him to the table. He called for his maids to dress the wounds and offered the man a breakfast. He just looked at the king and didn't say a word.

"I'm King Roger and—"

He was interrupted with a scathing, "I know who you are and what you are!"

"Good," replied the king. "So now we can concentrate on who you are, why you're in my kingdom."

"My reports state that you are from the far west beyond the Great Divide. I'm told you were a hard man to take down and managed to dispatch several of my warriors, some of them my best from an elite company on the western front. That's quite a feat taking on seven at once, let alone one. They are among the best-trained, most-capable fighters in the kingdom. I guess that's why I'd like to learn more about you."

"I am a simple trader of goods. I make my living helping travelers who wish to move west for whatever reason. From what I see around here, I can understand why they might brave the toils of the badlands to attempt a better life."

The woman administering the bandages had completed her job, and Jo-Eb thanked her for her kind service.

"Why would you thank a handmaid for her service? It's her job." The king was befuddled and somewhat annoyed.

"It's your kingdom, and you can do as you wish, but where I come from, everyone is of value, and courtesy goes a long way toward being civil."

The king shook his head. "You don't look like a dove, especially the way you fight—how is it you see value in a woman?"

"Well, since you ask, it's like this: there are two types of people in the world as far as I can tell. One seeks power and control. The other gets along quite well without it but uses it to his advantage when it's necessary. That way, you have fewer enemies to keep your eyes on."

They talked for the most part of the day and well into the night. The king decided he liked this Jo-Eb, so he wouldn't have him killed. He had to come up with something though to appease the warlord hawks to keep them in line. Since he thought so much of him, he explained his problem and consulted with him on just how to get out of this mess. Jo-Eb was puzzled, as a king's word is law, or so he thought.

As they discussed the issue, Jo-Eb inquired into the order of things and how one would come up in the ranks. The king explained that the most-proficient warriors vaulted to the top of the ranks and commanded the troops. Jo-Eb thought that a bit odd, as there are many people who might be great warriors but not necessarily good leaders. He surmised from that stance that very few, if any, of the members of the dovish clan were on the advisory council and surely not on the war department configuration.

"Sometimes a calmer head and a less aggressive attitude toward the completion of a process should be considered." He was offering his advice although the king hadn't asked for it.

He figured it wasn't presumptuous of him, as he was not a subject of the realm. Besides that, as long as he could keep him talking and interested, the more options he could have to evoke an escape. Although he rather enjoyed the interchange with the king, he was ever mindful that the king's will would be done at a flick of the wrist. With that in mind, he continued, "I've run across many types of men and women in my travels. Most are content to get by, but every so often, you come across an individual who has a great desire to impose his will on others. When that desire and energy is pointed at power to ensure that others are served, they are usually good leaders. On the other hand, when one desires power for its own sake, it usually leads to conflict and destruction. I wonder which of your subjects are content to obey the rule of the land and which desire to impose their own desires for their own glory."

The king just sat there as if in a trance for what seemed to be an extremely long time. "I've been so preoccupied with ruling I've forgotten the joys of the simple everyday life." He seemed to be talking more to himself than to his prisoner. I could cross the great divide and leave this life to those who enjoy the pursuit of conquest. Yet on the other hand, I don't think I'd make a good farmer." He slumped back into the chair, placed his feet on the table that the servants pushed into place, and exhaled a long mournful sigh. "And yet, as appetizing as it seems, it cannot be. I was born with a destiny, and try as I may, I cannot shirk my duties."

"I've set my mind to always do right, but…" He hesitated. "Who is to say what is right and what is wrong? My personal wish is to dismiss your case and banish you from this land, but then, on the other hand, I must keep solidarity within the kingdom. Where does that leave us?"

Again, he pushed his chair back, lifted his hands to his face, and rubbed the eyes as if he was trying to erase them from himself. "How can one lead the strong and display weakness, and how can one present a case that will cause the meek-minded to gather around and support my decision? Where is the justice in terminating a life for the sake of appeasement? Yet how do I skirt this without doing just that?" Once again, he pushed on the table that lay in front of him, first with a slow and steady grip then with a burst of "Uhh!" He violently shoved it clean across the room.

"Perhaps…," a low, shaken voice came from the lady in waiting. She stopped abruptly when she realized that she had dared to raise a voice in the presence of the king without being addressed. He scowled at her in displeasure.

"You dare to address…" His voice stopped in midsentence. He sat there silently for a minute, and then in a commanding look, he said, "Proceed."

"If your majesty would have him put in the dungeon, he would be available for further interrogation. I served your father and listened to his thoughts on many occasions. He always stated that the more you know about your potential enemy, the better off you will be when the fighting starts." She bowed her head and stepped back. The king's eyes lit up, a broad smile crossed his face, and he exclaimed, "Perhaps women do have a brain. Guard, take this man to the dungeon, see to it he is fed well, not beaten, and has ample reading and writing materials at his disposal."

"From now on," he indicated to the lady in waiting, "you shall be my council. I'm tired of the fools that fail to present any alternative position other than death or freedom. Yes, this will serve me well. The hawks will be pleased at their great leader preparing them for yet another battle, and the doves will be appeased knowing they have saved yet another life."

"If your league permits," the voice of the lady came again, only this time a little stronger, "I can see to it that the prisoner is properly taken care of and has ample opportunity to impart his knowledge for your benefit."

"Make it so!" He was elated that this issue was solved.

Once again, he turned to his breakfast, the one he missed yesterday. After finishing it, he called for his war council. He decided to expand the council to include a contingency from the Halcyon, which included Chun Leargas and two others from his clan, along with Jessica, his newly appointed member.

When Jagaren was called, he was full of exuberance that the king had not waited for the dust to settle at his feet so they could continue to do what they do best. His excitement was tempered when he saw the group that had formed. His manner demonstrated a great disappointment with the presence of the wimpy doves, and it seemed he almost choked when the woman arrived. "Surely, Your Highness, you're not going to let a woman in the chambers while the plans for conquest are laid?" His voice reflected the anger he felt, and he simply stood there in silence as if to demand an explanation from the king.

"Sometimes things are not what they seem." That was the only thing that the king gave in the way of explanation, and to him, the matter was settled.

"Now we will discuss our position, our plans for the immediate future, and a long-range plan." Jagaren was baffled at the thought of a long-range plan. After all, it seemed to him the plan was to continue to expand the empire. He had been informed that on the other side of the great divide was a land so vast that it would take years, perhaps decades, of engagement to conquer it. The plan then was simply to go on until he reached the vast ocean that he had heard about. He gave no thought to governing the territories simply to encompass them into the kingdom. Governing them would be for another generation once he had been laid to rest with honors.

"Now," the king started, "we will start with a review of where we are, where we intend to go, and how we expect to get there. We will start with the formation of our new supreme council. It has been related to me that perhaps the most senior and best qualified to lead in battle are those who are the most proficient in the skills of war. Those who are skilled at administrating the functions of the kingdom are best suited to oversee the events of governing the masses. With that in mind, I have decided to reconfigure the structure of the council. From this day forward, Jagaren is hereby appointed as my war general. Your responsibilities will include training, forming the battle plans, and conducting the method of war. Chun Leargas, you and your people will be charged with the responsibility of overseeing the administration of law and work jointly with General Jagaren to ensure his logistical needs are tended to.

"Now for those of you who have not been introduced to our newest member of the council, I present to you the Lady Jessica. I have declared her a lady and presented her with the status of Mistress of the Southern Lands. It seems she is native to that area and served my father for many years in the capacity of governess of that land. Today, I have bestowed upon her the title and the land that represents that area. Her official duties will be to review, consider, and make suggestions to my head administrative council"—he nodded to Chun Leargas—"on how to best govern that land in an attempt to tame it. This will serve as an experiment in transferring a wild, virtually ruleless land into a productive area to enhance the kingdom and foster a sense of belonging instead of revolution. Each, in turn, will retire for the next forty eight hours and, when summoned again, will present a plan to incorporate the new changes." He dismissed the council with a wave of the hand.

That settled, the king decided to review the training area. It had been a long time since he had time to just reflect on the building of the kingdom, and he wanted to be ensured that everything was in order. With that in mind, he ordered his new council members, General Jagaren, Administrator Chun Leargas, and Lady Jessica, to accompany him. While they were reviewing the court, Lady Jessica whispered in his ear that perhaps something could be gained from having the prisoner brought along to make observations. After all, he had dispatched seven of the best trained and was only downed by a force of twelve more who physically overpowered him. The king was leery at first as he considered the reaction of General Jagaren. He approached him with the idea of gathering information that might make conquest easier once they crossed the great divide. Lady Jessica proved to be most skillful in convincing the general of the advantages of knowing the enemy. With that, the king called for Jo-Eb to brought forth to accompany them.

As they walked through the training area, the king mentioned with pride at how he marveled at how well the training was going and boasted at the proficiency of the demonstration by the soldiers. Jo-Eb just shook his head and smiled. After seeing this, the king, visibly upset with his attitude, inquired why he was being so cynical.

"It's hard to believe that you would take pride in the accomplishments of a single person when others around are being beaten by their opponents," he replied. "Yes, with a vastly superior force, you may win the battle, but what of the cost?" He said nothing further, and the king scowled at the thought that anyone would be bold enough to question his methods.

They continued their tour in silence. Once completed, the king sent everyone back to their respective places, yet he determined that he would converse with Jo-Eb yet again. It was refreshing to be able to speak to someone who was not afraid to express an opinion. "Just why is it you are so critical of my training methods? What do you see as being wrong with training the soldiers to attain success?"

"You consider the value of the greater warriors, yet you do not give credence to those who are training to serve you and are put into the fight as pawns. So my question is, even if you have no regard for the lives of those soldiers, what is the cost in new recruitment, training, and providing armor and food to train new recruits when you could spend much less on time and materials on retraining those you already have?"

The king sat in silence again for some minutes. "So," he offered, "you think it would enhance my army if further training were provided to those already in service rather than to feed the masses to the enemy to wear them down so the real warriors can come and complete the job?" He paused as if in deep thought.

While he was contemplating this process, Jo-Eb offered, "Your first assault would be extremely more effective, and the expense of replacing your real warriors, as you put it, would not only improve the battle conditions but would be administratively effective. I like the way you think," the king responded.

With that, the king decided to have Jo-Eb moved from the dungeon to a room just down the hall from his. Its effect did not set well with Jagaren, but he held his peace in public for at least the time being.

4

"The king has moved Jo-Eb into a guest room on the same floor as himself. What an honor." Jagaren was relating his sarcastic remarks to his most-trusted advisors. The three, Marcus, Arrilio, and Mathisist, had served with him and under him for many years. He was at ease with relating his attitude in their presence, as he knew beyond the shadow of a doubt that they supported him a hundred percent. "This is an issue that will have to be dealt with in times upcoming, but for now, we'll let it rest." Having vented his frustrations, he turned his thoughts to coming up with a war strategy that would please the king when he was again called. "We need to be aggressive and push the western borders before they have a chance to muster an army. If the king don't dilly dally around trying to please the doves, we can cover a lot of ground swiftly and bring glory to the country."

The other three remained silent when it came to the actions about the king, as they wouldn't want to chance being overheard in what might be construed as planting the seeds of rebellion. Although each in their own mind would remain faithful to their leader, they personally held reservations about the other two. On the other hand, their reaction to the proposal to expand the limits of the country past the western boundaries was met with enthusiasm as the lust for blood speed through their veins. In this respect, they held nothing back, including raiding, plundering, and pillaging the country to the west. They discussed their options for several hours, and only adjourned at the supper hour. Jagaren was pleased at the progress and informed them that they would resume again in two hours. He didn't want to let the iron cool down.

When they returned, he informed them that he had worked out a plan that would place them in a bright light with the king and assure the failure of Chun Leargas to support the requirements to provide the administrative assistance and the equipment required to ensure success.

"I know that we'll suffer some heavy losses during the upcoming battle, but it will be worth it to demonstrate to the king that this new plan is faulty and perilous at best," Jagaren said. "We will sweep the entire western area in a matter of days and call for logistical support that he cannot ever hope to achieve. As for his Lady

Jessica, I have other plans. We'll send spies into the south land and stir up a bloodbath such as has not been seen for generations." His three lieutenants nodded in agreement with fire in their eyes.

Marcus responded that it could be a fool's errand if not handled properly. Jagaren cast a wicket glance toward him. "That's why I have selected you as the leader of the southern region project. I know you will not make any mistakes. You have proven yourself over and over again as a shrewd, fast thinker that can change course to take advantage of the unexpected. While the other two, as you, are great fighters and contain wisdom that I will need in the heat of battle, you stand far above the other two when it comes to quick wit." Jagaren laughed a hardy laugh and turned to his plans that lay before him on the table. Arrilio and Mathisist said nothing but looked at each other with questioning eyes. Jagaren didn't know it, but he laid a seed of discontent between the two and Marcus. Resentment fostered, and yet it was overlooked by both Jagaren and Marcus. At that, they turned to the plan at hand as Jagaren laid it out. Nothing was to be said of Marcus's separate task when the king was briefed.

Chun Leargas took his new obligation seriously, laid out his plan to determine the need of the kingdom, sectioned the vast empire into regions, and ordered a list of each that would provide for the availability of the needed materials in order to serve the king by establishing a network of resources and determining how much would be needed to support the war effort. In the back of his mind, he was sure that Jagaren would do all in his power to ensure failure on his part. Using that as a guideline, he started laying out a plan to present to the king.

Lady Jessica had plans of her own. While she supported Chun Leargas's plan in concept, she was sure that such a grandiose project would be years in the making, and her people needed relief now. Giving difference to his plans, she started laying out plans for adjudication and the appointment of local judges. She wasn't sure if the king would accept it, but she was confident that she could convince him of the wisdom of at least attempting the project her way. She also had plans for Jo-Eb. If she could convince the king that a more intellectual approach would serve him well, she was sure she could convince Jo-Eb to go along with her.

So each, when called again, presented their thoughts and ideas. Jagaren, of course, wanted immediate war to extend the empire past the great divide. Chun Leargas argued that the logistical support required would take months to prepare, and Lady Jessica held her tongue during most of the argument. She had reasoned that an insidious argument would grow louder and louder until the king would at last slam the broad side of his sword down on the table and declare that all this was getting them nowhere.

She was right, of course, and once he called the meeting back to order, she, in a very calm, mellow voice, asked to be heard. Since the king had placed a lot of emphasis on her being his new advisor, he waived his hand at the others around the table and, with a sweeping jester, pointed everyone's attention to her. Although she wanted to make comments on the others' plans, she knew that it would rouse up the others and the arguments would start up again. Steering away from the arguments about the war and logistical support, she mainly restricted her comments to the southwestern lands where she could have a direct effect in providing support to the kingdom. She managed to display a plan similar to Chun Leargas only on a scale that would be directed only to the lands that she now governed.

Since her spies had reported to her the intent of Jagaren to cause chaos, she attempted to avert that by requesting a contingent of warriors be placed under her jurisdiction for a short period. "After all," she commented, "these lands have gone on for quite some time with little or no jurisdiction, and until the subjects could be convinced that it was in their own interest to be protected directly by the king, it would seem reasonable that they would be suspicious of any attempts to establish a governorship led from the king's palace." She advanced that it was her conclusion that each branch of the council would be represented within her lands and each could be judged based on its successes.

The king noted that they had gone on for some time, and he had a lot to think over. Contemplating further arguments he dismissed them and set a new meeting for further details three days hence.

That evening, the king called on Jo-Eb to accompany him at supper. He was interested in Jo-Eb's views and what, if anything, he'd recommend. Jo-Eb, for his part, held his piece until he was directly questioned. "Well," he began, "it seems that you've put a lot of stock in Lady Jessica, so my suggestion would be to give her sufficient time to develop her plans into reality. As far as furthering the expansion of your kingdom to the western lands, you might want to consider that there are factions in the far southeast that have run freely for some time now. You indicated that those lands are responsible for the death of your father, and although they are labeled as part of the kingdom, they are actually rebellious and give no credence to your kingship."

The king once again stroked his red beard and looked at the cracks in the ceiling. "On one hand, I tend to agree with you." He paused and then continued, "Perhaps you want to gain time to warn the western lands about our plans."

"Without a doubt," Jo-Eb responded. "I'd send a warning in a heartbeat if I could."

"How is it that you can speak so boldly to one who holds your life in his hands?"

"Perhaps," Jo-Eb replied, "it's because I know you to be a seeker of truth, and the expansion of your kingdom will come in one of two ways. First, you can conquer the lands, but can you hold them? The second is to form an alliance where others will accept your kingship in a mutual beneficial treaty. That way, you can claim jurisdiction without the utter destruction of the land and its more important resource—the people."

The king allowed a slight smile to come across his face as he replied, "Once again, you have given more thought to the matter than most of my subjects. Yet I have an army that requires a continual sequence of battles, or I could lose the respect and allegiance of my subjects. I value the dedication of Jagaren and his followers, as we have fought side by side in the past and will do so again." He leaned back once more, stared at the ceiling, and then closed his eyes. After mulling it over in his mind, he simply said, "Good night."

Jo-Eb departed for his room. As he was returning to his quarters, he met Lady Jessica in the hall. From her movements, he could tell that this was not a chance meeting, so he followed her to the great hall where they had a snack delivered.

"What do you have in mind?" he quizzed her.

"Not much for social talk, are you?" she replied.

Then as they snacked, she laid out her idea of how he could be of great assistance if she could convince the king that he should go along with her but he would have to give his word that he wouldn't try to escape. He simply smiled and replied that it was one promise that he couldn't give. "I don't break a promise, and that's why I wouldn't agree to it. You know as well as I the plans he has for my land and that I'll do everything in my power to prevent it."

She left him in short order with the comment, "Well, perhaps it's something you can mull over. I know I could use your advice, and perhaps you could think of something that would be of benefit to both of us."

He sat there for a long period, trying to decipher the code. He concluded that even though he couldn't make a break for it, perhaps he could get word of warning to the other side. He didn't make any public statements or write anything down as he knew that his continued existence depended on the disposition of the king. After thinking on it for a period, he simply returned to his quarters.

Early the next day, he was summonsed again to the king. "It seems you've gained quite a following," the king started. "First, the Lady Jessica has asked for your assistance, then Administrator Chun Lergas has requested that you be allowed to accompany him on his tour of the kingdom, and lastly, without any fanfare, Jagaren has request your presence in order to help retrain the less effective of his troops. Yes, you've got quite a following."

"With respect to the desires of the others," Jo-Eb intervened, "I'd sooner not be a part of any of their official duties. Each has their own reasons for wanting me close. Lighting's desire, I believe, would be to see me killed in the heat of battle, as I'd be honored with great fanfare, yet his objective would be accomplished. Both Administer Chun Leargas and Lady Jessica would require me to give my word that I would not try to escape, and that I cannot give."

"So what do you suggest?" The king seemed to be in short temper, but since he asked, Jo-Eb replied, "Simple, just let me go, and I'll go back to my land. The next time I return, I'll either go around you or bring back an army to defeat you." The king broke out a roar of laughter. "Yes, I imagine you would. And that's exactly why I can't let you go."

"So I remain your prisoner even though I must admit your hospitality is most gracious. As I explained to the Lady Jessica last night in the great hall, I can't give a promise I don't intend to keep."

The king looked quizzically at him for a minute.

"Surely," Jo-Eb continued, "you knew of our meeting in the hall, as I was returning to our quarters."

"Yes," the king replied, "I know of it and even what was said."

At that point Jo-Eb injected, "The lady has only your best at heart and will give her life to support you if it comes to that." He paused then continued, "If only everyone had the same commitment." He said no more as he could see the king's face flushing a bright red.

With one final thought, Jo-Eb added, "It's not for me to judge. I am fortunate enough not to be the king."

That seemed to defuse the situation, and the king once again just shook his head. "What am I to do with you?" The comment was more of a self-spoken thought than a question. "We'll speak again later. For now, I want to take a long ride, and I'll call for you again later."

Jo-Eb got up, and went back to his readings. His motive was to learn all he could about the king and the way this land worked. He'd learned much in the short time and had the insight to know when he was pushing the right buttons. Since the king had given him free reign in the library, he made sure to use it as often as possible. *"Know thy enemy,"* he said to himself. *"Find out what drives him, what he likes most, and what, if anything, he fears."* Searching for clues, he pulled out the archives, starting out with the oldest manuscripts.

"You spend a lot of time in the library," commented Chun Lergas. "Tell me, what do you find so fascinating about those old manuscripts?"

With precise movement, Jo-Eb pushed the book back slightly and cocked his head toward the door. "Well, you're a quite one, aren't you?" he replied. "I've been looking for the history of this civilization, and where better to look then the library?"

Chun Lergas seemingly making idle conversation responded "I see you have three books set off to the side. Surely, you don't plan on reading all of them today, do you?"

"Oh, those, no, I've already looked at them. The first three, there are exact duplicates of the ones in our library in Kentucky. I didn't find any difference even in the verbiage."

With a confused look on his face, Chun Leargas stood there in silence. He had that look of amazement that Jo-Eb had seen before. "How can that be?" he finally asked.

"Well, I didn't find any books further back, and as with most archives, the majority of the stories were exactly the same, starting with a period just prior to the great light period. I was really hoping that perhaps I'd get some insight on what might have happened prior to that period, but it's not here. I really was more hopeful than expecting anything different."

Chun Leargas quizzed him about the archives in this place called Kentucky and asked how the manuscripts could be so closely related. Jo-Eb explained that prior to the devastating attacks that broke up their civilization, this entire continent was united under one flag. It was called the United States of America.

"And who was the king of this land back then?" Chun Lergas asked.

"No one," he replied. "The government was formed as a republic and had fifty states. Each state had their own state government, and each relied on each other for the safety of the entire nation."

"And just how big was this United States?" he asked.

"From what is now called the divided waters of the Atlantic to the Pacific Ocean. Back then, they called it the Atlantic and Pacific Oceans and the country consisted of forty-eight contiguous states. In addition, we had two other states: one called Alaska, the furthest one north on the western border, and one called Hawaii, which at the time was some three thousand miles off the West Coast."

"I've heard rumors about that but never thought it was true until now," Chun Lergas exclaimed. "So what do you expect to find now?"

Jo-Eb told him that he'd like to gain some insight into how and when the divide occurred after the great light. "It just seems to me that somewhere along the way, organized law under our constitution fell apart, and I'm just curious as to how that happened and, once the dust settled, how the new governments formed. Since I'm a captive here, I have nothing else to do but see if I can't put some of the pieces back together."

With that, Chun Lergas turned slowly as if in deep thought. Then he turned back again and said, "Perhaps we can research these together sometimes." He turned again and briskly walked out of the room.

Jo-Eb shrugged his shoulders and, without giving it another thought, went back to his research.

He'd been sitting there quiet for a spell, just thinking of how things had seemed to be all of accord, and with that one catastrophe, it virtually wiped out an entire civilized world.

"Chun Lergas says you're studying the old archives." It was a quiet voice, and he recognized Lady Jessica immediately. "Yes," he replied, almost as if in a trance. "Yes, and it depresses me to think that at one time, we all had the same goal. Yet in one short period of time where the entire world went crazy because one group wanted total power over everything, we almost lost it all."

She smiled briefly and replied, "Well, is it any different now?" She paused only for a brief second then continued, "You have the haves and the have-nots. Those who are seeking power and those who want to hold on to it. I've read most of the history, starting with the twenty-second century until present date, and the story is always the same. The powerful want more power, and the greedy want more of what the powerful have. I wish there were an answer, but I'm afraid it won't be in those books. They all end the same no matter where you are from."

Jo-Eb reflected on this for a minute then responded, "Yes, but it don't have to be that way. For instance, where I come from, we do not have the wars that you here experience. For the most part, we have managed to pull ourselves back together again and live in peace."

She responded, "Hum" with a slight smile on her lips. "And you do not have any quarrels about who owns what and how much is enough? No one ever draws a sword or shoots an arrow at their fellow man? Yes, you people handle the problem with a little more finesse, but the motives are the same, and I have no doubt that if push came to shove, each side would line up against each other and fight."

"Well, if you put it that way, I guess you have a point."

Then she proposed that they should work together to see about what form of peace they could forge that would satisfy both sides. They discussed it for the better part of the day, and when suppertime came, she invited him to join her. He graciously declined, as he had a lot to think about and didn't want to inadvertently tip his hand. He had no illusions about her loyalty and always kept that in mind when talking to any of them.

5

The next day while he was reading, he heard some commotion in the long hall. He stopped to see what he could glean from the commotion. He observed three soldiers dragging a young woman down the hall, and she was yelling that once Jo-Eb found out about this that he'd come and cut their guts out. Once he heard his name, he called for the soldiers to stop for a minute. He was wondering who might be using his name and how he would be involved in this. "Who are you, girl?"

"Jo-Eb," she screeched and then sighed with relief. "Tell these hooligans that I'm a free woman and not their slave!"

As luck would have it, the king was just departing his quarters for the breakfast hall and stopped to see what the commotion was all about. The three soldiers immediately knelt down and replied, "Your Eminence, this hellcat has killed several of our solders and destroyed many animals and supplies."

The king looked at Jo-Eb and asked, "Do you know this woman?"

"All I know as of now is that she was being dragged down the hall and called my name. If you will allow me, I will endeavor to see what I can find out."

The king was intrigued, so he waived to him to continue.

"State your name and your reason for calling mine," Jo-Eb commanded.

She looked up with a smile and responded, "Barbara, Arabia's sister. I was passing through this land on my journey to New York when these baboons attacked me and slaughtered my horse."

Jo-Eb turned to the king. "Yes, I know her, and I believe she is telling the truth. Her sister Arabia was a close friend of my wife, Jana. We've spoke of her briefly and some of my history. When I last saw her"—he pointed to Barbara—"she was just turning thirteen and had a desire to go east to see the sights of the large cities along the Atlantic coast. I'm sure she meant no harm."

The king raised his eyebrows and simply replied, "Now I've got two to contend with. Clean her up and bring her to me. Jo-Eb, we'll all meet for supper tonight and see what can be done about this." The king turned to the guards. "Treat her as a guest. If any harm comes to her, it will be on your head." Satisfying himself that this quick decision would relieve the immediate pressure, he turned back, and offered Jo-Eb to attend breakfast with him.

"What's this all about?" she asked Jo-Eb.

"Take your time, clean up, and we'll have a chance to speak later. Do not offer any intent, and only respond directly to questions without elaborating. Do you understand?" The emphasis on the last statement resonated throughout the hall. She briefly looked as if she was going to raise an objection, and then in a flash of light, she caught on. They escorted her to her newly assigned quarters, and four maids attended to her needs.

"Jo-Eb, Jo-Eb, what am I to do now?" the king said. "Now I have two to contend with, and if things accelerate, we'll have an entire castle full of guest." His last statement reflected a matter of concern and was that of someone truly dismayed. "Well, we'll have to consider this matter. In the meantime, join me for breakfast."

Jo-Eb couldn't help smile as he detected a man with a real problem. On one hand, he wanted to do the right thing by them, and on the other, he needed to do the right thing to maintain his support. "Tell me something of yourself so I can understand how I am to proceed." The king was shaking his head as if in disbelief as he asked the question. Jo-Eb relayed that he'd been in the great library and had discovered that the first three books were almost identical to the books he'd had access to in Kentucky and the archives of the last place he had been involved on the other side of the great divide. "They all seem to come from a common origin. It supports the idea that we were all at one time gathered under one civilization and governed by the same set of laws. After the great light period and the breakdown of law, we gradually formed our own systems to meet our individual needs."

"So tell me about yourself. Tell me what you are made of and why you think. I am charged with governing a very large land over a thousand miles in each direction, and I wish to govern it wisely."

Jo-Eb just sat silent for a couple of minutes. He wanted to be able to speak to this man, as he considered in his own mind that this king really wanted to ensure his kingdom was fruitful, but he also knew that a person in his position would be ruthless when necessary. "Okay," he responded at last. "I'll tell you what I can." He went on about his younger years and his upbringing. He related how he had initially taken on a mission to find his cousin for the sake of his aunt. The king had been sitting there for the better part of two hours just listening quietly. It seemed that he felt whatever else he had to do was secondary to his learning the history of Jo-Eb and his experiences.

Then without warning, the king got up, pushed the table across the room as he had done so many times before, and let out a bloodcurling yell. "Why do I listen to the ramblings of a foreigner? Where is it written that a king should take advice from not only a man without a title but also a potential enemy?"

Jo-Eb responded calmly yet forcibly; "A man who claims a title also claims the responsibility that goes with it. I have no title, yet I have led men both into battle and across deserts and mountains where the natives fear to tread. Also, I do not view you as an enemy. Yes, if the day came and we had to fight, I'd stand my ground against what I view as tyranny and oppression of the people." He paused. "Yet I don't think that day will come. You are a wise ruler, and I believe that sanity will prevail."

The king slumped back into the chair, placed his feet on the counter where the books are laid out for examination, tilted his head back, and stared at the ceiling. "If only it was that easy." His voice was barely audible, and Jo-Eb could sense the pain that was flowing through the king's veins.

"Enough for now, we'll talk again later. Enjoy your time in the library. I wish I could sit beside you, but it's not to be." The king's demeanor changed. A smile came to his face, and it was almost as if he were a different man. He waived Jo-Eb off in a nonchalant manor and called after him, "Have a good day."

He returned to the archives and spent the entire afternoon browsing the old manuscripts. He found not only the development of this civilization and its governing structure but also many references to battles and the lessons learned from them. Several of the old, dusty manuscripts that hadn't been touched in generations listed detailed accounts on how to train for war, how to take advantage of lack of the enemy who was not prepared to meet the onslaught of a massive army, and how to best deploy troops. He made no mention of them when he spoke to others, as he valued the information as a most valuable tool. Since he'd been an avid reader from the many years of practice when his aunt Martha insisted that he learn to read well and given the fact that he was taught by the elder of the library how to speed-read, he found it rather exciting to be able to absorb and retain volumes of data. Now his training was paying off.

Just as he placed the last volume back on the shelf, Lady Jessica stopped in to watch and see how he was doing. "Are you enjoying your quiet afternoon?"

He smiled back and responded, "I find it fascinating to study the culture of a country especially when so much of it mimics the books in our own libraries. For instance, were you aware that with the exception of the spelling of some of the names of the heroes of old, the accounts are almost verbatim. For instance, the story of Indiana Jones in some books refer to him as a hero of his people while other books hold him to be a traitor to his country. In one of the few references to individuals prior to the great light period, a man by the name of George Washington was held in high esteem by territories that are now sectioned off and ruled by the powerful, yet the story is held to be absolute in its context. The only difference is that the name in your history books refers to him as George Wellington. Both individuals actually existed, and both were famous in their own right, yet in our history, Washington was the first duly elected official to rule the country while Wellington was a famous general and a great leader of men. So it would only be natural for the hawks to pay homage to him while the doves would hold Washington in higher esteem."

"Do the books mention weapons of war? I understand that the weapons used were much more advanced than what we have today. For some reason, those weapons have not reappeared."

"Not yet," was his response.

"Not yet."

As they were talking, an attendant entered the room and announced that the king had need of her and that she should go post haste.

Jo-Eb enjoyed talking to her, as she had a pleasant manner and always seemed truly interested in what he was thinking. While he did enjoy her company, he always reminded himself that she was the eyes and ears for the king and that she wasn't slow to catch on to things. So he always kept that in mind while talking to her. He was convinced that she meant him no harm, yet she would turn on him in a heartbeat if she thought he was planning something that the king wouldn't like. He had to admire her for her honesty and loyalty, yet he knew that any slipup would be met with a harsh response. With that, he spent the remainder of the afternoon meandering through books that had nothing to do with war.

As evening fell, he was once again called to the king's council room, and when he arrived, he found much to his surprise not only the king and the three members of the council but also Barbara. She was seated in the far corner of the room, not physically chained but notably not part of the conversation. It was about her but not with her. As he entered the room, Jagaren was speaking. He was giving a rhetorical speech where he would make an accusation, point to Barbara, and demand that she be punished severely with death for her outrageous actions. He paused for only a couple of seconds when Jo-Eb entered the room to scowl at him and then continued, pointing at her, "Your Majesty, this infidel cost us the lives of thirteen good and faithful warriors. It took us nine days to corner and capture her, and even then, she managed to wound three soldiers, severely cutting off the ear of one." His frustration was clearly evident, and his answer as always was to cut off the head.

After he finished his report, he looked exasperated. Once he had been quiet for several seconds, Chun Lergas spoke up, "Given what you say is true, why then do you wish to kill one so competent? What is it that this one young woman, not even out of her teens, as you say, has what our warriors do not? Shall a person be put to death because they are more adept, stronger, faster, and shrewder than the opposition? I use the same statements and line of thought that I had when I advanced that we not kill Jo-Eb, as although we may view him as the enemy, perhaps we can learn from him."

Just at that moment, the supper feast arrived, and the king motioned that the papers should be taken away for a while, as he was going to enjoy his supper and wanted no arguments while the food was being served. He beckoned for Barbara to come forward, and the servants brought her chair to the table. "We will dine in peace!" And that was the final word while the meal was being served. There was some small talk, and Lady Jessica mentioned to the king the facts that Jo-Eb had relayed to her that afternoon. For his part, Jo-Eb did not make a big deal of it. He did not want to get dragged into a confrontation and drive any wedges between the parties at the table. So when the king asked him to relate the story as he had relayed to her that afternoon, he kept it as low key as possible. He said that it seems that two great leaders have somehow been rolled into one story and that each in their own right had a place in history. Then he added, "Since that was over eight thousand years ago, I'd imagine that some things have been turned around and even left out." The king seemed satisfied and left it at that.

As the meal concluded, the king turned to Barbara and stated that now that all had time to digest the events of the recent past, he would allow her to speak. This was a most unusual position to take, as the only ones who were empowered to speak to the king on matters of policy and decision making were normally members of his council. Jagaren started to pose an objection but was stopped dead in his tracks with a stern disapproving look from the king. He closed his mouth and sat back down.

Barbara began by acknowledging that she had eluded her pursuers for several days. With that, she started her tale. "I was traveling alone across a desert land when I was first approached by a small band of five individuals who inquired as to why I was here and what my intentions were. I replied that I was simply traveling through the area on my way to a place called New York City. They attempted to restrain me, so I dispatched them, killing three and running off the other two.

"A short time later, a squad of six of your soldiers accosted me, saying that I was a member of a rebel group and was to be brought in for questioning. I didn't cater to this, so I animatedly objected, and the results were that I sent them into flight. I killed one, wounded several others, and disarmed the remaining ones. I told them to go back to their camp and report to their chief that I am not an insurrectionist and have no intention on staying in their territory any longer than was necessary.

"On succeeding days, I was pursued again and again, and as a result, I killed more soldiers. I didn't like killing, but they wouldn't quit. Your recorder there"—she pointed to Jagaren—"stated that I killed thirteen and maimed several others, but what he did not tell you was that on at least three occasions, I sent the wounded back to their camps even though I knew that I would perhaps have to meet them on the field of battle once again. On the last occasion when I was finally caught, it was because three of his brave soldiers deserted one who was severally wounded, and despite the fact that I was fairly sure that I'd get snared, I assisted the young man back to his campsite. I've heard no more about him, but I hope he is able to recover."

The entire room was deathly quiet for a long time. The king just sat there for a while, taking it all in. "And you swear this to be the truth?"

"I'd not lie to save my life," was her response. "What's done is done, and facts cannot be changed by insertion or omission."

Jagaren squirmed while trying to muster a defense. "Surely, you don't take the word of an insurrectionist over your faithful servant?"

With that, the king waived his hands for all to leave and replied, "I have much to think about this. That is all for now."

As the group got up to leave, he motioned to Jo-Eb and Barbara to remain seated. Once the room was cleared, he once again addressed Barbara, inquiring her to repeat parts of the story. He had the leader of the squad who was in charge of the final episode brought in and, without making any comments, instructed him to relate the events of that day. The squad leader bowed deeply before the king and begged that his life be spared.

"What am I to condemn you for? Are you not the one in charge when this person was captured?"

"Yes, sir," was the reply. "But I did not order her to be taken. It was the captain of the guard who issued the order. I simply obeyed the orders as they were given to the best of my ability."

The king motioned to him to get up and ordered that he proceed.

"Your Eminence," he continued, "we did what we were instructed to do but did not demonstrate hostilities towards this person. The young boy she saved was my younger son, just recently trained. This was his first battle, and although she had inflicted the wounds, she also administered to his welfare right before my eyes. I had a struggle within me. While following the orders, I was also grateful to her for her kindness. I have no reason to believe that she is other than what she claims to be." With that, he bent to one knee and raised his sword in a display of support to the king, as was the custom.

"Bring me the young man," was the king's command.

"It is not possible, sir, as the commander of the troop had him executed that very day for aiding and abetting the enemy…" His last sentence trailed as tears welled up in his eyes. "Better that I had been killed that day instead."

The king motioned to his servant. "Have this man returned to his home without harm." With that, he dismissed the man. "How can one expect such loyalty as these events unfold?" His comment was more to himself than to the others.

"If I may, Your Majesty?" Barbara injected. "The man who just testified before you swore allegiance to you on this very spot despite his love for his lost son. I am not one to attempt to correct the ways of your kingdom, yet I feel compelled to state that the account of these events leave me in great doubt as to the sanity of the person orchestrating these events."

The king blurted, "You think that you have the right to council me on the affairs of my kingdom?" His anger was obviously not in control, and he half drew his sword from its scabbard. "Should I not put you to death on the spot for speaking without permission, let alone questioning my head of war council?"

She stood her ground and replied, "You are free to do what you think is right, and if that cost me my life, then so be it, yet you can't deny that something is amiss in this room." She remained seated yet never took her eyes off the king as she made her case.

"Perhaps," Jo-Eb chimed in. "Perhaps it would be a good time for a break." His voice was mellow and southing yet also was spoken with an air of confidence.

"Let it be so," replied the king. "For now, return to your quarters while I muddle over this issue." With that, they both left his presence.

As they walked down the hall, Jo-Eb commented that if she was going to keep her head, she might try a little finesse. "The truth matters," he told her, "but what good is the truth if you're no longer around to enjoy the results? Never deviate from the truth, but always remember that an emotional outburst from one in his position, although he may later regret the action, won't do you any good if you are dead."

They came to her assigned room, and she entered without a response. Jo-Eb continued on to the library.

6

Once again, Jo-Eb sat in the great library with its many manuscripts. This time, he concentrated on the art. He observed that many of the original paintings recaptured the early days of the empire and that, in many cases, the faces of those being described were blurred to the point that they couldn't be recognized. In the more-recent ones, the facial expressions and likeness were even more obscure than those of the past. He wondered about that and determined to ask if and when the situation arose. It appeared to be a deliberate mutilation of the paintings rather than one of original intent.

Along with that, he noted several manuscripts that were placed directly out of order on display so he decided to check into this and began reading the content. He didn't get very far when he was interrupted by a furious elderly man, apparently the keeper of the room who was screeching wildly and flailing his arms in a most-erratic manner. Jo-Eb was momentarily taken aback at this and retreated several steps toward the door when he was joined by Lady Jessica.

"Mr. Barbosas!" she called. "Please, he is our guest and does not know the significance of his actions. Please settle down and calmly explain to him why you are so upset."

The old man instantly dropped to one knee and replied, "I beg your pardon, my lady. I was only aware that he had access to the outer regions of the room. I will, of course, explain." In an apparent awareness of his position with regard to the lady, he somewhat timidly addressed Jo-Eb, "Sir, I ask your forgiveness in this matter. Please do not be offended, but in my excitement, I failed to control my emotions. You see, what you have lifted from its place is considered holy ground and can only be touched by a curator and then only with the proper sterile gloves. Everyone who is a member of the realm knows the matter and the penalties for violating the current law."

He continued for several minutes explaining the value of these relics and the determination of the keepers to preserve them in their current state of being. He finished with a deeply regrettable account of his unexcused actions and asked that his punishment be swift.

"What does he mean his punishment?" Jo-Eb inquired. The lady replied,

"The establishment of our class structure is such that no one can raise an objection or their voice to a duly recognized ward of the king. Even if the case is a mistaken event, the fact that it took place requires retribution. As a result, he must be punished."

"And what is the regular punishment for a violation of this matter?" Jo-Eb feared what he was about to hear.

"A sentence of a slow death would be the appropriate response. Of course, it is up to the one who has been violated, in this case, you."

He had a hard time believing his ears. This man would be flogged to death for attempting to safeguard the law? "What kind of justice would that be if a man such as himself were punished for attempting to protect the very thing he is charged to protect? How can I influence this issue?"

She looked at him strangely as if he was asking for absolution for the man. "You can, of course, request an audience with the king and present an alternative if you wish. But I wouldn't advise it."

Without hesitation, Jo-Eb proclaimed that it was his intent to address this issue with the king. He had thoughts of clemency and perhaps even a reward for his faithful service, but that was normally not to be.

Shortly, he was called before the king and indicated that he knew of the obligation that the king was under, but in his opinion, punishing a valiant server of the king was not an act punishable by death. The king appeared to be extremely agitated at this encroachment on his evening. Nonetheless, he was a stickler for protocol and called for them to appear immediately. First, the old man presented the facts as he knew them and as they were, then Jo-Eb had the opportunity to inject his comments. "Your Eminence," he started, "I have wronged your servant and inadvertently broken one of your laws. Let there be no harm come to this your most faithful servant who has provided protection over a most cherished artifact of the realm. If punishment is to be administered, let it be on my head and not on his." At the conclusion of that brief statement, he returned to his position and sat down.

The frustrated king waved for all to leave as he considered this matter. Everyone except Jo-Eb immediately rose and departed the room.

"Was I not clear when I said everyone?" The king pointed his finger at Jo-Eb. "Have I not made it abundantly clear that I need time to consider this and that I would do so in private?" His voice was clearly raising, and his eyes flashed in a manner that Jo-Eb could swear that fire was coming out of his eyes.

"Yes, sir," he replied, "but this is an issue that not only concerns the king and one other man—it's the foundation of the entire civilization that you have created and needs to be considered calmly and rationally. If I were to depart now, I would be placing you in a most precarious position. On one hand, the law of the land is what it is, and you are the administrator. On the other, the law has been in place for several generations, and what might have made sense a thousand years ago may no longer be appropriate." He sat there as if not expecting a response but hoped that the king would see the logic in it.

The king slipped back in his usual position, propped his feet on the table, leaned his head back, as he was inclined to do when he was in deep thought, and said nothing. After a bit, he offered, "Just what would you propose I do? It is the law of the land."

With that, Jo-Eb spoke again, "There are many types of rulers in this world. Some are arrogant fools who do things because that is the way they are while others much more wiser have the ability to reconstruct matters to their advantage. They get the best of both worlds. On one hand, they have a beacon of knowledge passed down from one generation to the next, and on the other, they have the opportunity to display true leadership and compassion for their subjects."

After a pause, the king pushed forward, placed his right hand on his knee, and stroked his long red beard. "Perhaps you are right. Assuming that you are, I will have to consider how to impose this as a lesson learned and demonstrate both leadership and total command. I have decided. Have everyone in the council and the curator brought back in."

In short order, everyone was back in their places. Lightning had come prepared with a set of irons and an attendant who carried the whip and the chains with which to perform the punishment. Brighter and Lady Jessica sat, silently watching the proceedings. The old man was placed on his knees before the king.

"I have decided on the course of action that this situation will occur. The laws of our land were written thousands of years ago when the country was unstable and the future of the empire was in jeopardy and chaos was the order of the day. During that period of time, kings dealt harshly with those who opposed him and showed little consideration for his subjects. This time has passed, and now we must advance our civilization by making some fundamental changes to our laws. As the king, I am charged with ensuring that our nation remains strong. That is why I have chosen Lightning to lead our glorious armies. I have confidence that he will prevail in every case and that he, without reservation, will do what is best for the kingdom. On the other hand, I will not tolerate willful disregard for the violations of our established laws. Therefore, I decree that any future incidents of this case be brought before me or my appointed council for dispensation. As I do not, as of this minute, have an appointed member, I will administer this matter as I see fit. Therefore, it is my decision that the violator of the law be turned over to the violated for justice as he sees fit. Therefore, in this instance, Jo-Eb will declare the proper disposition of this matter as he sees fit." The entire room stopped as if frozen in time. Not even a breath could be heard.

In short order, Jo-Eb rose from his position and stated, "Since it is my responsibility to impose punishment in this matter, I have decided that Mr. Barbosas will be banned from the library for a period not to exceed seven days. It is his most prized possession, and to deny him access for that period of time will ensure that anyone contemplating a violation of the king's law will suffer the loss of that which is held most dear to him. I could think of nothing that will grieve Mr. Barbosas more than to deny him the opportunity to diligently serve his king. Since I do not wish to impose a shock to his system, I am directing that he and his entire family be taken to the village of his youth where he will have time to contemplate the folly of his actions." With that, he sat back down.

The king, with a broad smile on his face, responded, "It is as it is and will be forevermore. Mr. Barbosas and his entire family will be properly provided for, and he will start his punishment as soon as he can get his affairs in order."

Later, Lady Jessica was speaking to Jo-Eb about the matter and asked how he determined the action that he should take.

"It was simply a matter of being innovative," he responded. "While I'd not had a lot of time to consider this issue, I had been notified that Mr. Barbosas was going to ask for a delay in his death and be afforded ample time to return to his home of his youth and get his affairs in order. I was also informed through the books that I've been reading that it was customary for the convicted to make such a request and that under normal circumstances, it would be granted. Since that period usually lasted for a period of seven days, it was only right that his punishment be met during that time. Once completed, he will return to a useful service as he has been doing for forty-some odd years. Yes, I believe this worked out well."

Early the next morning, Jo-Eb was called to the king's chambers. He wasn't prepared for what was to happen next. The king started, "I've been giving some thought to your presence here and what to do with you, Now to top it off, I have a second one of you that is just as puzzling and even harder to control in my mind because she is a woman." He sat there in his usual manner, leaning forward slightly, stroking his beard, and staring of into Neverland. He sat there silent for several seconds that actually seemed like an eternity in the eyes of those assembled. Gathered in the room was the war chief Jagaren, the chief administrator Chun Leargas, the lady Jessica, Barbara, and Jo-Eb.

"I, as the king of this land, am charged with ensuring that my kingdom is solid, safe, and continues to grow. Although I am inclined to dispatch leniency whenever it suits my ends in this case, I have determined that the personal joy of encounters is outweighed by the needs of the empire." He sat there again for a long time and stared at Jo-Eb and Barbara. Finally, he commanded, "Those two are to be returned to the dungeons. They will be treated with respect and honor of that given to any defeated king or queen, and they will no longer have the freedoms of the castle." In his usual manner, he waived his hand, and the guards roughly took hold of Jo-Eb and Barbara. "I said with respect!" the king bellowed. If you don't know how to respect another, just think of them as your child. You will not beat them nor will you deny them as much comfort as you would like to expect in your own home. Do it now!"

The guards unhanded the two and, in a slight dip, extended their arms toward the door. They were allowed to gather their few belongings and led to the outermost part of the castle in the deepest part of the jail. It was three stories underground, yet it had been constructed with a series of mirrors that were angled to allow light into the place during the day. They were placed in separate cells although the internal doors to their rooms were not locked. The fact of the matter was that even though they were in a dungeon, their living quarters were not much worse off than the rooms that they had been staying in the king's floor. There was plenty to eat and drink. There was even wine and fruits and nuts. Each room had been constructed so as to give the

— Jo-Eb's Quest —

appearance of privacy with extended comforts provided for a well-respected guest. Only in this instance were they obviously not guests but prisoners.

"What do you suppose brought this on?" Jo-Eb inquired.

"Well, I suppose it's my fault," she responded. "I was approached late last evening and instructed to report to the king immediately. Since the hour was late, I took more time than actually required before I was ready to report, and when I arrived, King Roger was furious. 'How dare you to make the king wait!' His voice was almost a crescendo, and his face was as red as his beard. I tried to respond with dignity and attempted to defuse the situation by remarking, 'I dare not cross the king, Your Eminence, yet would you have me appear before you naked?' My attempt at defusing the situation only made it worse. He kicked the table across the room as he often does, then he paced the room for what seemed a never-ending circle. Finally, when he did stop, he looked at me with questioning eyes. I couldn't determine if he wanted to ask me questions or give me directions. Finally, he stated that he had made a final decision in my case. He stated that he was going to marry me off to Jagaren and I would present many fine young men for his future army. I, of course, objected to the plan and responded that if that was his intent that he should take his sword and run me through to get it over with fast or, if he preferred, he could consign me to a dungeon for the rest of my life. In any case, I will not marry until I am ready and then to the person of my choice." She stopped for a second then said, "I suppose that lit the powder keg. I didn't think he'd include you in this though."

"It'd seem only natural that he would include both of us, as we pose, from his point of view, the same threat." His response was more reflective in manner of a man in concert with her view than with any sorrow or self-pity. "Look at it this way, he could have chosen to put us in chains with beatings three times a day or, worse yet, had us killed on the spot." After a few seconds, he continued, "No, I don't think he wants us dead, as we have a lot of potential value to his cause. The fact that he enjoys our company is simply a plus for both sides. We get to remain alive, and he has the potential of learning new ways to govern and extend his conquest. We've simply got to keep in the front of our minds that although he is congenial enough, his direction and allegiance is to his kingdom, and personal comforts must be placed aside in order to accomplish his end goal."

Jo-Eb requested permission to have books brought from the library so he could continue his pursuit of knowledge and even extended an offer to Barbara to join him in his research. He didn't hear the decision of the king for several days and thought perhaps he had declined his request or more likely had not received it.

The king was a powerful man but also held them in respect. That was obvious from their quarters. Although they were officially prisoners, he had demonstrated that his kingdom came first and his will was to be obeyed without question. In his decision making, he always tried to leave a back door open. Finally, after seven days, he was presented with a paper and pen and instructed to write down the books he wanted to sign out. He was doing his research in the sixth millennium and requested social, religious, and edicts from that period. His objective was to keep his request as broad as possible in order to dissuade any thoughts of his being involved in a covert plan to disrupt the current government structure.

Since they had nothing else to do, Barbara just watched him for a couple of days almost without interest. She was apparently deep in her own thoughts and gave no indication that she would join him. After a while though, she came to him and explained that although she was interested in what he was doing and thought it would be good to gain an understanding of her enemy, she, quite frankly, would be of no use to him, as she couldn't read. "And," he quipped, "I was born with a book in my hand? Reading is not a natural-born ability nor is it a sign of intelligence—it's simply a matter of opportunity and the desire to learn for a greater purpose."

"A greater purpose?" she responded. "What do you mean?"

"Well, we all have choices to make in our lives, and the choice to learn to read is one that has a potential payoff that exceeds many of the other possibilities that life has to offer. If you know your enemy, you are in a better position to take advantage of his weaknesses. I can teach you to read, and since we've got nothing but time on our hands, I'll have you reading in no time at all."

She smiled, took one of the books from the stack, and stated, "So let's do it."

They spent the next couple of weeks reading, writing, and discussing ideas. As it turned out, she did have a modicum of reading experiences, and her ability to catch on impressed Jo-Eb to the point that after the first week, he mentioned that he thought she had been putting him on when she told him she couldn't read.

"No," she replied, "I was not playing games with you. I honestly did not think I knew how to read. But after just a few hours of practice, I discovered that I can place ideas into sentences and sentences into paragraphs. Another thing that has helped is that the writings in these old texts consist of strings of old English and not in the Eng-jarg that is so often used today. I was taught to read English as a child although the books that I had available were not quite as extensive as these. I still have trouble with the words that I don't understand, but when you explain their meanings, I'm able to remember them. Many of the words are written often enough that once I know them, I am able to recognize their content and meanings. Actually, it's been fun learning to read and not at all as scary as I thought it would be.

7

One day while they were reading the manuscripts, Barbara ran across the name of Jo-Eb. She thought this was amazing that his name should appear in the lineage of this kingdom, as its spelling was not common even in today's world.

When she asked about it, he replied that his name was a conjugation of two identical twins, Joeb and his brother, Ebenezer. Jo and Eb had spent most of their lives together, and when he came along, they joined the names as a symbol of their everlasting devotion to each other. It was a mutual point of interest, so they decided to pursue it to determine what connections it might have to him. As it turned out, the Jo-Eb of the sixth millennium was among the greatest chiefs of the warriors in that age and actually served as the cornerstone of today's strength as a nation. History and genealogy were of prime importance in that day, so they were able to trace the heritage all the way back to the great light period. As Barbara continued reading, she made mention of the recordings.

"According to these records, this nation was actually born out of the remains of the survivors who were driven out of Kentucky during the great light slaughter." As they continued their research, they discovered that their hero of old, Indiana Jones, had a brother by name of Ebenezer, and through his efforts, the basis for the foundation of this new world was founded.

"Why would the inhabitance of Kentucky want to drive out the brother of Indiana Jones?" Barbara queried.

"You've got to remember that although many folks of that day gave Indiana a place of prominence in their lives, there were also those who thought of him as a grave robber. They attributed the war that ensued on the story that he had defiled the tomb of the great leaders of the east. Their hatred of Indiana also extended to any of his family and many who did not flee in time were killed," Jo-Eb explained.

"It wasn't until several centuries later when the dust settled that the true version of those events came to light. As it turns out, we are actually cousins many times removed from this current-day nation," he continued.

By this time, both Mr. Barbosas and his sons had been making it a normal routine to check on and even conduct research with them, and they expressed an unusual interest in this as it developed. Mr. Barbosas never failed to repeat the story of his unusual punishment and felt indebted to Jo-Eb for the opportunity to get away if even for only a short period of time. Once the discovery was made pertaining to the link, the curator endeavored to ensure that the information would get back to the king. He never spoke of it while around his family as he feared repercussions from the general. He knew beyond a shadow of a doubt that General Jagaren would do anything to keep this type of information from the king. So he worked quietly and suppressed his enthusiasm for the project.

One day while they were all researching the archives, Lady Jessica quietly slipped into the dungeon area. She always made sure the guards had something special to keep their silence while she was looking at what was happening in the cells. She heard Mr. Barbosas speaking of how odd it was to think that perhaps the king and Jo-Eb's families were of the same lineage. His older son Robert, happened to see a shadow in the outlining area and silently raised his fingers to his lips. All knew what it meant, so they went silent. After a couple of seconds, Robert replied that although at first he had thought the same thing but upon closer examination, he discovered that the names simply sounded alike but the spelling was different. Barbara shrugged her shoulders and murmured, "Yes, you're right. The spelling is different." With that, they changed the subject and went on as if it wasn't a real big deal. The letter *b* in the word had a tilde inserted on it.

After they were sure that she had left, Robin, the next older son, let out a deep sigh of relief. "You think she bought it?" he said.

"If I know her, she'll be looking through the old archives to check up on you," Jo-Eb stated as he gently rubbed the back of his neck.

"Don't worry," Mr. Barbosas stated. "I keep two sets of books, unknown to most people, so I doubt if she'll get a hold of this one. I started that many years ago when the castle was under siege and always kept the old copies stashed away in case. Now, I suppose, it's a good idea that I did." They all smiled, and you could see the relief on their faces.

Sure enough, not two days later, Lady Jessica came down for an official visit. During her discussions, she mentioned that she had been following Jo-Eb and his companions in their research, and while dong so, she had run across a section where his name was mentioned.

"Yes, we thought that odd at first, but it's spelled differently, so we just discarded it as an oddity and haven't given it any more thought," Jo-Eb replied.

She seemed to be happy with that explanation and went on with her visit. Since she had been coming down on at least a weekly visitation since they were placed there, it didn't seem odd that she would be checking up on them. Jo-Eb knew that she had an ulterior purpose for her visits but always managed to keep the conversation on the light side. On this occasion, after a while, she said, "Don't you want to get out of this place? I can't understand how you can just be so calm about being cooped up here. Yes, it's nice, almost as nice as where you were before, but you're still in a dungeon."

Jo-Eb smiled and asked, "Got any suggestions? No, I don't like it here, but I can't do anything about it either. Perhaps when the winds of politics change, it will be for the better."

"If only you'd agree to not attempt to escape, I could gain more favor in the king's ear," she replied.

"You know I can't do that. My word is my bond, and I'll not lie to gain favor of anyone. No, the king will just have to have a change of heart and decide that I will honor my word not to try to escape if he takes me out of here."

After she left and things went quiet for the evening, he pulled the dressing chest away from the wall and continued his work. He and Barbara had been secretly chipping away at the wall behind the chest and had a rather substantial hole in the stonewall. It was very slow work, as they had to ensure that all the pieces were small enough that they would not be detected as they broke the stones loose. Most of it was ground and simply spread as dust. Barbara had managed to convince the guards that it was very dusty down in the hole and was allowed to use towels and water once a week to wipe it up with. Some of it was placed in the privy and carried off, but in every case, they were sure to pulverize the rock so it wouldn't give them away. What they had found was that even though the cells were below ground, the mortar that held the stones together were soft and pliable due to the age of the structure.

The visits continued, mainly from Lady Jessica, about every other day. Jo-Eb was coming suspicious that something was happening and was considering how he could make inquiries without causing an uptake in the awareness factor while talking to her. On one occasion while she was visiting after only a short period of time, she made a startling statement. "I suppose you don't know—being cut off from most of the outside world—but things have been happening around here."

"Yes?" was his simple reply.

Then she continued, "The king is away with his war general." The contempt in her voice when she mentioned Jagaren was pronounced, and she didn't attempt to cover it up. "It seems there has been a rebellion in the southeastern corridor in the province of Saint Michaels in the country formally known as Arkansas. They are protesting the severe treatment of the citizens of that region by Jagaren and his men. His general"—again, her contempt was blatantly obvious—"has convinced the king that it is an all-out uprising and needs to be dealt with, with a heavy hand. They have been gone for a couple of weeks now, and I expect they will probably be there the rest of the spring and through the summer. Recently, I have received word that a contingency of three hundred of the king's far western border had encroached on the far west across the great divide. They were met by a contingent of armed mountain men headed up by a man known only as HW and a partner Jebedia. Only six of the king's men were returned. They were stripped of their armor and only had the bare minimum to survive on and returned to their own camps."

Jo-Eb and Barbara couldn't help but smile and then laugh out as she related the story.

"I know them both," he said as she looked quizzically on. "Both are great leaders, and both will deal harshly with any further incursions. Given that your war general is away and won't be able to fight on two fronts, I guess his war party will have to wait another year or two before attempting to cross the great divide again."

At that point, she broke into his conversation. "No! He has a large-enough army to wage two wars at once, and his second in command, Marcus, is as ruthless as he is. If I know Jagaren, he will convince the king that he has plenty of men to conduct two battles at once. I expect an army of twenty-five thousand are now being gathered to pursue your friends." Jo-Eb frowned at that thought. *"Well, in my current circumstances, I don't have a lot of options."*

At that point, she interjected that she thought it was a crime that that war mongrel would get away with it, as in a long run, it would be damaging to the kingdom. She was prepared to make an offer of a temporary allegiance with him. If he would give his word that he would not try to escape, she would send messengers to his friends so they might be able to prepare for the oncoming invasion. "I don't do this lightly," she commented. "I see this as an overall plan of that war general"—she wouldn't even state his name—"to overthrow our king and establish himself as the king. I believe he will take advantage of any situation that may endanger our king, and I wouldn't put it past him to kill the king if the situation presents itself."

"What is it that you'd have me to do?" he inquired.

"If that scoundrel is successful, he will upend my position and lay waste to the southwestern region that I am charged with. If I am able to thwart his plans, the king will return safely, and I will be able to do for my region that which I promised I'd do. I'd make the area safe for the peasants and generate a new culture that will thrive and swear allegiance to the king. That was my promise, and that is what I intend to do. But…" She paused. "I won't be able to do it alone. I'm counting on you for help. It will help both your people and my king if you will agree to not attempt to escape while this is going on."

Jo-Eb pondered the words and their meaning for a few minutes and then replied, "I will work with you." Barbara had been sitting quietly, just listening to what was being said. She was somewhat taken aback by Jo-Eb's agreement but held her peace. "Good," Lady

Jessica replied. "Now I need something from you that would serve as a sign to your people that what I am going to tell them is in fact true. What do you have that you could use to present this to them so they will know that I speak the truth?"

Without hesitation, Jo-Eb responded, "Send my emissary. Barbara will take the message to them, and they will know that what you are saying is true."

Without hesitation, Lady Jessica responded that it would be impossible, as she couldn't know what the girl would say. Jo-Eb responded, "It's the only way that this will work. The last anyone from that region heard from me was when I was in the land of the green people, and as far as they know, I was killed in an earthquake and swallowed up by the ground. How it came to be that I escaped death is a story for another time, but if you are going to convince them that the roomers of my demise are incorrect, you will have to have a firsthand report from someone they trust. Barbara is the only one who has seen me since that episode and is the only one they will accept as being truthful. So, you see, your plan will not work without sending her."

Barbara started to make an objection. "Well, nobody has asked me what I think! I don't care a hoot for your kingdom or your region, and I purpose you let both of us go, and we'll promise not to invade your land and kill you and your king in return." Her voice was such that it took no interpretation as to the meaning of her threat.

Jo-Eb simply replied, "Yes, Barbara, that's possible, but think of the number of people who will be killed in the process. I think this would be a better idea, and it will save lives of our comrades." He just stood there looking at her, waiting for a response. Her eyes lit up, and she simply nodded her head in the affirmative. "So be it."

Jo-Eb stated as he looked at Lady Jessica, "The next move is yours."

After what was actually only a few seconds but seemed like an eternity, she agreed. "Okay, Barbara will go, and you will promise not to try to escape." With that, she turned to the guards and stated, "Take this one," referring to Barbara, "and see to it she has provisions for her journey. Seize that one"—she pointed to one of the guards—"as he is a spy for that war general and would betray us." The other guards hesitated for a couple of seconds, and then one stated, "In the name of the king, I demand that you release your weapons!" He pointed at the guard in question and pronounced that his allegiance was with Lady Jessica for the benefit of the king. They took the guard away to another dungeon and chained him to the wall. "He must be restrained at all cost. Do not allow him to speak with any other guards or prisoners, for his venom will spill out and contaminate others. If he yells, gag him." Satisfied that she had covered all the bases, she turned again and said, "Remember I have your word." She motioned to the guards. "Move this one back to his original quarters. I will accept personal responsibility for him." She glanced at him again and said, "We will talk about this again. I have some plans, and you will be involved in making sure they are carried out." Without further comment she quickly turned and left.

Jo-Eb and Barbara gathered their things and started on their new series of events. "How is it you think they will believe me?" she stated. "They don't know me, and they surely don't know that you are truly alive."

"Tell them," he responded, "that HW is a great warrior, as was his forefather from New York, and tell Jebedia that I still grieve over the loss of my beloved whom he presided over at the wedding. They will know you are telling the truth."

With the wheels being set into motion, they separated, and each embarked on their own separate missions.

The next morning, Jo-Eb was briefed that Barbara had left the castle and was headed for the great divide. Lady Jessica insisted that she be accompanied by a contingency of one legion to guard her against any possible rebels that might object to this meeting. The lady knew that she had a trusted ally in her confidence, *Rasmussen una dedicata* (the dedicated one), who had pledged his loyalty to the lady Jessica. He had met Rasmussen on a couple of occasions and was confident that Rasmussen would do all in his power to protect her. She had made a comment before leaving that she would feel more secure if they would allow her to proceed on her own. After all, she had been trapsing over the countryside for two years now, and until she ran into the unfriendly king's men, she had done quite well on her own. The lady, however, insited that she did not want to leave anything to chance. Barbara reluctantly agreed to the escort, but in the back of her mind, she had resolved to dump this excess baggage at the first opportunity.

As for Jo-Eb, he was determined to find out as much as he could about the current state of the king's health, for he feared that perhaps Jagaren Lightning may attempt to take advantage of any situation that might arise and had no doubt in his mind that Jagaren would attempt to overthrow the king and assume the kingdom for himself. He made it a point to contact Mr. Barbosas, as he was sure the librarian was totally committed to the king and would do anything in his power to ensure the king was able to continue his reign. As it turned out, the idea proved fruitful, and their joint efforts forged an even tighter bond than had existed before. Chun Leargas had gone with the king's army to ensure a continued stream of supplies and weapons were available for the ensuing war. Jo-Eb was confident that Chun Leargas would align with the king, but he was not confident that he would have enough power to persuade the king that Jagaren was to be watched.

Being mindful of their precarious situation, he arrived at the conference table where Lady Jessica had called a meeting. He wasn't sure just what she had in mind, but he was sure that she was counting on him to be a man of his word and that he would assist in any way he could. "My word is my bond," he stated as he entered the room. He observed that there were several people in the conference that he knew but also there were some he had not seen before, and he wanted to leave no question as to his intent, so he continued, saying, "I have given my word to the Lady Jessica that I will not attempt to escape while I have been given free reign of the castle. I wish to add to it that although I am not a subject of this kingdom, I have found your king, Roger, to be an honorable man, and I have committed myself to his service while he is not presently available to run the affairs of state. For any who might doubt my integrity, I offer my sword to his service for this period." All eyes had been trained on him and now shifted to the lady for her response.

8

Without further comment, Lady Jessica rolled out a map on the conference table. It had several areas that had been annotated by different colors in specific areas, and she hesitated for only a minute then went into her idea. "We've been a nation under one king for several millenniums now, and I have sworn my allegiance to this king. I will not yield on this, as I have sworn to support my king, and my word is my bond." The inference could not be missed, and everyone knew that she accepted Jo-Eb as an integral part of her plans. She allowed all to scrutinize the layout for some time without comment. Finally, she continued, "As you can see, I've identified some areas of grave concern to the protection of the kingdom and our king. While I do not make any accusations about anyone in particular, I'm sure that each of you has heard rumors about turmoil being generated for the sake of affecting a takeover and the overthrow of our king. I have been temporarily presented with the job of ensuring the castle, and thereby, the kingdom is protected. I do not take this assignment lightly and have reasons to suspect that there are certain elements within these very walls that are dedicated to the overthrow. Our mission here today is to ensure that the castle is safe and the nation is secure until our king returns."

She paused again and receded into the background as the members scrutinized the map. After a short deliberate delay, she continued, "As you can see, I have selected a region in the southwestern region where we will establish a temporary headquarters. The objective will be to build a fortress where we can provide the king with sufficient shelter to enable him to regroup in the event things do not go as planned. Those of you that are here today have been handpicked based on my observations of your expressed loyalty to our king. As many of you know in recent days, Jagaren Lightning has made overtures that have many of us worried that he will attempt to overthrow the king and proclaim the kingdom for himself. I have been able to obtain reports from my spies to this effect and have strong reason to believe that an attempt is only days away." She paused for a moment then continued, "I'm not sure how much the king may know of this, but I have attempted to reach him without success. Now are there any questions?"

"Yes!" came a loud reply from the captain of the guard Eckerd. "Why is this man allowed to be in this conversation, as he is a prisoner of the king and surely not to be trusted?"

"He is a man of his word and has presented to me that he will not attempt an escape while the king is in jeopardy and furthermore will provide assistance as he is able. Unlike some of the kings' men, he is honorable and will abide by his word."

Someone in the back stated, "He'd better, or he'll be holding his head in his hands."

They looked toward Jo-Eb, and he simply responded, "I have spoken."

Lady Jessica continued, "Okay, now that is settled, it's time to get to work. I have sent a contingency ahead to start gathering the resources for the building. By the time we get there, we should have enough materials to construct this fortress quickly. As I mentioned, I don't know how much time we have."

"I also have a question." This time, the question came from Robert, Mr. Barbosas's oldest son. "How can you be sure that the peasants will not attack while we are building this fortress? The area you have selected has been a wild, lawless area for centuries, and the king has never been able to tame them."

"While what you say is true," she continued, "I have been there no less than six times in the past few months. While they have expressed no undying love for the king, they are aware of the presence of General Jagaren and the suffering that he would impose if he were able to unseat the king. No, they do not love our king as we do, but they have enough sense to know the results of a coup. They will assist!" That last part was spoken with confidence and reflected a sense of contentment on her part. After all, these wild men, as they were described, had come closer to being a part of the nation in the past six months than they had in the previous several centuries.

The lady assigned Eckerd, the captain of the guard, to oversee the castle in her absence. He had two lieutenants who each had a legion of one thousand men plus the castle guard of three hundred and the palace elite consisting of no less than one hundred well-trained, handpicked soldiers. No other army could muster such a force to present an attack on the castle. Once all the preparations were made, they set out in haste to the areas that she had assigned. She was confident that all would be well in the event the king had to be escorted, yet an uneasy feeling prevailed. There was something that she was missing; she just knew it. Something that keep her awake at nights and a gnawing feeling that something was going to happen that she could not control.

The march took seven days and six nights. They rested for only short periods, and she ensured that the guards were doubled at night. She knew she had done everything in her power to ensure this success, but she still had that eerie feeling that something was not right. Toward the end of the seventh day, the site designated on the map came into sight. She could see the workmen constructing the fortress as she had lain out, and at first glance, it seemed that everything was in place as it should be. For some unknown reason, she halted the column, dispatched the army that she was leading into an offensive position, and motioned for the rows of soldiers to precede slowly at the ready and with caution. She couldn't place a finger on it, but something was not right.

Jo-Eb came up and offered an observation: "There are campfires placed on all of the high mountains completely surrounding this site. It looks as if they have attempted to put out the fires in those areas before we would recognize them. If you haven't already, I'd dispense four squads to circle the outer perimeter so they can be approached on both sides if necessary."

Lady Jessica smiled and quietly dispatched massagers to complete the defenses, and then with an unfurling of the flags, she took the lead position in the direction of the main camp. In what seemed forever, the procession headed straight on. The soldiers positioned and slowly inched forward, closing the circle ever tighter. When they were halfway to the front gate, a contingency of about one-third of the soldiers reversed course and formed a blockade to ward off any attacks from the rear.

As expected, once the garrison flying the flags got close enough, the arrows started flying. The shields went up over the lady, and an impenetrable shield was formed. Slowly, ever so slowly, the covering was moved back until those in the party were a safe distance and could not be harmed by the onslaught.

The battle raged on throughout the night, and at dawn, the sight of bodies sutured the grounds. Although Lady Jessica was not directly in the fracas, it seemed that she was everywhere at once. Her orders barked out as that of a seasoned commander, and her resolve reassured the troops that victory would be theirs in the end. She had a white flag posted and sent a message to the garrison, stating the following, "Your situation is untenable. You have not had sufficient time to lay in gross quantities of reserves to last for more than a week, and the fortress is mainly made of wood. I will listen to your concerns. However, I can and will burn your buildings to the ground in less than a day. If you wish to roast, just stay where you are. Otherwise, agree to meet with me. You have one hour allotted to make a decision. After which, I will commence with the fire brigade." She placed the insignia of the king on the seal and had the messenger carry it to the opposition. As a display of her sincerity, she had the fires lit just outside the arrow range of those held up in the fortress and ordered her best longbowmen to position themselves just beyond the reach. Her strategy for negating any surprise attack from the high grounds worked out well also. The reports came back that casualties from the four squads was light, and as the enemy had not expected such a ferrous counterattack, their numbers had been routed and would pose no further problems.

"You have proved yourself worthy of any experienced field commander." Jo-Eb made the comment while waiting for an answer.

"It's not my first rodeo," she replied. "I've been in many scrapes when I was a young rebel commander against the king. Once I was captured and stayed with King Ruper, King Rogers's father, for some time, I became a loyal supporter of this kingdom as a nation. His father wanted to expand his regime far and wide but not because he enjoyed conquering land and people. He did it because he wanted it large enough to present a formidable buffer that would protect the subjects of his kingdom. Few understood that well, and even fewer were concerned with the state of the subjects. Jagaren never understood that and has only one thing on his mind: conquest."

At precisely the one-hour mark since they had no response from the besieged camp, she ordered the longbows to prepare for an initial blow. The lieutenants were positioned so that they could hear the command and see the red flag as it was hoisted and, on the prearranged signal, let fly the initial volley. They were set up in a four-depth attack and offered relentless voiles one after another. In short order, the white flag appeared from the fort, and the order to ceasefire was given. A message arrived with an offer to surrender. It had bloodstains on it and was fared at the edges with burn marks. "Looks like we've made short order of this battle," Lady Jessica commented. "Instruct your leaders to present themselves within the hour, and I will listen to their concerns."

Nothing further was said as the rider returned to his masters. Shortly after the rider entered the fort, a small contingent of soldiers followed by officers of the battered command came out.

The tents had been pitched, and the headquarters was laid out with full military attire, and the flags of both sides were placed in order to give credence to the word of the lady that she would listen to their concerns. As they arrived, she had them greeted and led away to their quarters for remainder of the day. When a few demanded to speak to her right away, she sent a reply that the day was late and there had already been too much bloodshed on this day. One of the opposing officers stated that the day was young and the noon hour had not even arrived yet. She gave no direct reply, but let the word get out that the representatives would be afforded comfortable quarters and time to refresh themselves. That way, they would be ready for the meeting the next day. Lady Jessica had purposely set up this scenario to demonstrate that she was in charge.

The opposition wasn't happy about it, but they were in no position to argue either.

The next morning after a prolonged delay featuring a lush breakfast and an hour of entertainment, the two sides met.

"Tell me," she started without hesitation, "just what are your concerns and how do you purpose to present them." The tone was set. It was obvious that she was not going to entertain any threats or cajoling from the other side. She spoke quietly without a display of emotion but firmly. "Just what problems do you have?" After a moment, one of the junior officers stepped forward and presented himself as a spokesperson for the entourage.

"We are representatives of the general Jagaren. His command was to disrupt and destroy any attempts to set up a fortress in this region. He assured us that we would meet with little, if any, resistance and were to report back to him as soon as the matter was settled."

"Do you have any proof of what you are saying, a written document perhaps?" Lady Jessica was careful not to let her feelings for the general be displayed, as she wanted to be able to ascertain the very nature of this act. "It seems the general has mistaken this effort as a rebellion against the king when, in fact, it was established for his very protection."

The officer seemed confused at first. Then with his wits gathered, he stepped forward and proclaimed that he had a sealed document with the insignia of the general that any attempts to establish a fortress in this region was to be thwarted at all cost no matter who may attempt to do so. He presented the document with the pride of a successful soldier who had completed his mission. After the report was given, the lieutenant stepped back, saluted, and returned to his place in line.

9

"We have gathered here this morning to obtain the reason for the distress of the people of the local area. What we've found is an invasion by troops sent by the general to ensure that this area is controlled by him. He has not been given the authority by the king to perform this action, and it is a clear violation of the king's dictates. Now we are faced with not only protecting our king but to quell a very decisive action on the part of the general to establish direct control of this region." Lady Jessica wanted to make it clear that her statement to her subjects who had sworn allegiance to her was in the name of the king. "My first question to this assembly is with whom do you place your allegiance? Mine is directly to the king, and I will do all in my power to ensure that he is safe. The second question is to the representatives that have obviously come to destroy our efforts and establish a dictatorial control over this land. To them, I present this question:

why is it a junior officer is acting as the spokesperson for this group? Why have I not been addressed as is established by protocol by the senior ranking member? You have laid a plan of deceit and destruction, and for this, you shall be punished. Take all but the officer who met with a response and place them in the make shift prison that we have."

To the one officer left standing, she stated, "I commend you for your bravery and your honesty. Because you had the intestinal fortitude to complete your mission, I am releasing you back to the compound with instructions for those remaining in the fort to throw down their arms and align themselves outside the gates. Those who do will be offered sanctuary within our confines, and their fate will be met with kindness. For those who refuse, I will utterly destroy the very place where they now stand, and they will be killed as opponents of the king. You have two hours." Having impressed upon the patrol that had attempted the ruse, she turned again to her assembly. "Now we will make contact with the local people and establish a peace so that they are aware that we are here for their protection." She assigned several massagers to be dispatched to the neighboring communities with the invitation to attend an upcoming summit. "Come." She motioned to the remainder. "We have a lot of work to do and only a short time to complete it.

Later that day, they received a message from the castle that word had arrived that the general was wounded in combat, but his wounds were not serious. The report also stated that the king had ordered one of the remaining legions to advance toward the area where he was conducting his summer battle. One legion had left in compliance with his orders, and the other was placed at the ready in the event they were needed. This report did not seem to bother Lady Jessica, as she had been involved in many campaigns over the years and was aware that troops were often sent forward to reinforce the battle-worn and serve as replacements for the casualties. She was happy that she had the foresight to leave a large-enough contingency at the castle to meet this demand if and when it came would be available to be dispatched.

After the allotted two hours, the lady emerged from her tent. "Have the troops assembled outside the gates as I demanded?" she inquired.

"Yes, Your Ladyship." was the response. "It seems that all have laid their swords down in front of them and are standing awaiting your instructions."

"Good. Have them to file in front of our camp. Tell them to separate into two groups, one on the left that desire to return to the general and his war and one to the right for those who wish to remain and serve our king here under my command. Be sure to instruct those who wish to return to the general that no harm will come to them from me and they will be free to choose without fear of recrimination." Her orders were repeated, and the soldiers were marched forward. Most of them moved to the right. About a hundred had moved to the left, and they were given their weapons, clothing, and equipment for their return march, and their wounded were attended. As they prepared to leave, the lady addressed them, "I know that you are true and loyal servants of the king, and I send you off to serve him as best as you may." To the junior officer who had stepped to the right, she addressed him, "I know you are a true and honorable man and servant of the king, so I have a special dispatch for you, one to be presented to General Jagaren and the other directly to the king. I caution you not to let the general know of the second dispatch. I fear that he may have plans that are not in the best interest of our king."

He placed the messages into his pouch, stepped back, and rendered a smart salute. "Your word is my command," he stated. To the returning troops, she bid a fond farewell with instructions that the lieutenant had been assigned as their temporary leader until they have returned to their units. They accepted her orders without comment and started the long journey back.

She called for Jo-Eb, and upon his arrival, she inquired of him of his thoughts as to the events of the past day.

"Why do you ask me?" he responded. "I am but a prisoner and have no direction to give. I will obey your orders, as I have given my word, and will honor my intent not to attempt an escape."

"Yes, but I have not brought you along as a prisoner but as a consultant. I have observed you, and you are a man of honor and also of wisdom. I welcome and even direct that you consider the happenings and provide insight for future plans that may occur. It's a precarious situation to be in, on one hand to know that you are a prisoner and subject to the whims of those in charge and yet to be placed in a position of trust. What I know that you know is that if that general is successful in his attempts to overthrow the king, your life will be cut short without so much as a mention of your existence. If it's any consolation, I'll wind up in the same boat." Her smile was one of both knowledge and concern. There was no doubt in her mind what would come of her and her beloved region if he were able to overthrow the king, and she had convinced herself that it was in his plans.

At this point, she stated, "Enough of this idle chitchats. I know that you are not only a great warrior but also a leader of men. You will act as my spokesperson to the local tribe's representatives, and it will be your job to convince them that it is in their interest to support my cause in order to protect their own lands and families."

He replied, "You've spoken so eloquently. Why do you need me?" He could see the smile on her face and the gleam in her eye.

"I am from the king's castle, you are an independent, and they will more readily listen to you than to me. In the end, I'm sure we could both attain the same results, but you will get there faster and relieve me for other business that I must attend to."

He admitted to himself that her logic was simple, straightforward, and sound. Considering all that she needed to do it was a logical move on her part. He started to prepare to act as the host of the gathering of the clans.

She directed that the work on the fortress be continued, and a new set of exterior walls were placed outreaching some one hundred feet from the original. The exterior walls were made of mud clay and were seven feet thick. There was no doubt that it would be a monumental task, but she had determined that the original fortress was only a scale of the actual fortress to be established. Since there were very few huge stones to be used to build the walls, she had directed that a clay factory be built to provide for the protection of the inhabitance. It was obvious from their initial assault on the initial construction that the wood, although it would be satisfactory for the interior, would not stand a chance of providing any form of reasonable protection when assaulted by a standing army. This standing army is what she was preparing for. It was her hope that they would have enough time to fortify themselves before the onslaught if it were to come.

The lady had sent a message back to the castle to inform Mr. Barbosas of her concerns and cautioned him to gather around him as many troops as loyal to the king to ensure that if the general actually was able to overthrow the current king and returned to the castle that he and his family would have adequate time to make their escape. The rider returned in less than seven days. He had made the round-trip with the help of three horse stations that had been set up by the locals. With that, he was able to keep a fresh horse at his disposal at all times and could ride straight through. When he reported back to Lady Jessica, he had a message that Mr. Barbosas had convinced the captain of the guard that the remaining legion was to stand in alliance with the king, and if the king was actually in danger, he was sure in his own mind that the general would know of her proceedings and would not return to the castle. If, in fact, he was successful with his plot to overthrow the king, he would head directly for the new fortress. With that in mind, he had convinced the captain of the guard that reinforcements would be needed at her place and the castle would still be adequately guarded.

Once he insured that the castle was adequately protected, the captain ordered three-fourths of the legion to proceed to help her defend the new fort.

He maintained that with the 250 of the legion left in place along with the castle and the palace guards that there would still be a sufficient protection left for the castle. He also stated that his job was to protect the library and its contents and he would remain at his post. He could see no reason for the general to take out his anger and frustrations on a librarian. After all, he concluded, no matter who is in charge, the great library provides direction for our future generations and must be guarded.

While Lady Jessica welcomed the thought of the new troops, she couldn't help worrying about Mr. Barbosas. She had grown fond of the old gentleman and his family. She dismissed the massager and instructed him to get some much-needed rest. She had the thought of stationing some other riders along the route to enable them to stay fresh, but she worried about the wisdom of entrusting these correspondences to people who may or may not remain loyal to the king as the wind blows.

To come up with some alternative methods of solving the problem, she decided to call a small contingent of the officers together and present the communication problems to them to see what they might consider a reasonable strategy. While they were in conference, although Jo-Eb was not made part of the team, he requested an audience. This aroused her curiosity, so she allotted him time to make a report. As it turned out, the very reason for their meeting was the answer to the problem. Jo-Eb reported that despite the fact that the various factions were not fond of each other and had reservations about aligning themselves together that he had been able to convince them that their current state would be much worse if the general was able to overthrow the king. With that as a common bond, they had agreed that although their local differences still had to be ironed out, they would be much better off cooperating for the benefit of the entire region then continuing their infighting. He had managed to convince them of their joint interest and that whatever may come, they must hang together or surely they would hang separately. The wisdom of the ages have come back to roost. He offered that rather than setting up the three stations that were relatively indefensible that a more secure method would be to have the riders proceed from one town to the next. It would be a longer route but would serve as security and would still be quicker than the three stations due to the number of horses and riders available.

One of the junior officers offered that normal communications could still be used on the more direct routes and that only highly classified communications would be used for the second option. That way, if the general had any spies—and he was sure he had some—the report would go back to the general, and if he attempted to interrupt communications, he would not know of the secret method of sending messages.

"Every time I think that I have covered all of the bases," she commented, "I am amazed at the latitude of intelligence that comes from this command." After considering several of the options it was decided that secret routes would be set up as suggested. Everyone seemed to be enthusiastic about the decision and was thankful that they had been included in the meeting. So it was established through Jo-Eb that several towns would be included and that alternate routes would be established so as to present a challenge to anyone attempting to make sense of it.

Lady Jessica called her initial trusted rider to formulate a pony express and establish control over that contingency. She sort of felt bad that she had not included him in the decision to provide an alternate route for the highly classified documents. Her reservations proved to be beneficial later on. She continued to supervise the building of the garrison and arranged for traps to be established in the flatlands to deter any aggressors from that direction. While they were proceeding, they received a message from Mr. Barbosas with plans that he had extracted from the archives for catapults, both stationary and movable. She directed that several be established in strategic places to help cover valleys and between the mountains to cover the passes. She directed that most of them be movable to enable the defenders with the ability to redirect them as needed. For those set up in direct defense of the fortress, they would remain stable but had the ability to maneuver 180 degrees. With three on each corner, they would provide a formidable weapons system.

In the meantime, Jo-Eb continued to mediate with the elders of the local towns and managed to iron out several of their differences. Once while in a meeting of several of the elders of the towns being represented, he relayed his story. He told of how he came from across the little divide from a place called Kentucky. He told them of the story of how he had gotten started on his quest to find his cousin and how over the past several years that he had covered much of the lands from the far north cold country where ice made up the ground to the area so far to the south that he had observed the remains of the great canal that once joined the two oceans together. He stressed that although he is an independent man, his mission right now was to assist them so their lives would be better and perhaps offer the opportunity for some of them to seek a better life elsewhere. The thought was beyond imagination for most, but he knew that a few would think on it and perhaps one day decide to follow in the pursuit of knowledge and enable them to become part of the spread of civilization once again.

When they asked why he had come to this land, he simply responded that he had never given up on the idea of finding his cousin, but in his travels, he had made many detours. When he relayed the story of the people who lived beneath the ground and featured a green glow, many thought that he was simply spinning a yarn to attract those who might think of him as a hero and that he was simply building his own prestige. Surely, the elders said that this could not be. Yet in the back of their minds, they wondered. When they pressed him about the green people, he explained that they were the reemergence of a people of long, long ago who had lived, died, and survived the direct exposure to the catastrophe of the hydrogen explosion that contaminated the entire region, and that after mutation and several generations, they had become accustomed to the environment. He had simply experienced it in his travels but somehow was immune to the deadly effects of what they call radiation. He explained how he had come to first observe its deadly effects and how because of his wife's insistence that they stay to bury the dead that he became aware of the inhabitance. Later, after his wife had passed away, while working on a trip that he might find his lost cousin, he returned to the area and eventually established not only a relationship with them but grew rather fond of them as a people. He was toying with the idea of settling with them for a while when a great tragedy struck.

The final thing that he remembered was that he was exploring a cave in the hope of finding artifacts that would link the green people to the rest of mankind when a great earthquake struck. He remembered getting struck on the head, and that was the last he knew of until he regained consciousness. "When I awoke," he continued, "at first, all was pitch-black. I wasn't sure if I was still alive or if I'd died and went into the afterlife. I thought surely if this is my eternity, I'd gone wrong somewhere and was condemned to eternity in solid blackness. I prayed out to God to provide me with an answer and to allow me to understand. I don't know how long I was out, but I couldn't hear any sounds, and I didn't even know if my eyes were open or shut. It didn't seem to make much difference. After what seemed to be an eternity, the ground shifted again. At first, it was a slow-moving action like sitting on a rowboat with no ores and the gentle breeze slowly pushing me to shore. After a bit, the ground trembled more violently and heaved like huge waves during a storm. I was caught in a chasm and was not able to reach very far in any direction. When the turmoil stopped, I thought I saw a very faint red glow from afar. At first, I thought that God had punched my ticket and determined that I was not to get out of this. I contemplated my end and decided that if I was, in fact, going to get out of this place, I'd have to do something.

"At first, I was only able to crawl, then with the passage of time, I was able to get upon my knees and finally to my feet. I staggered like a drunkard, as my balance was precarious at best. I was able to steady myself by holding on to the side walls. They weren't very far apart, so I could position myself in the center and proceed toward the red glow. After a bit, I noticed that the red was getting brighter and the atmosphere seemed to be hotter and breathing became harder. In short order, I was able to figure that I had been going toward a lava pit, and although it was not moving at a rapid pace, it was headed in my direction. With that, I decided to climb up and away from the area. From the books I've read, I knew that the lava contained poison that would fill my lungs, and if it were to catch me, I'd be consumed by the burning sentiment. At that point, the thought crossed my mind that perhaps I was in eternity and would be consumed forever and repeatedly by the fires of hell. Again, I turned to God and ask if I had fallen short of his grace and if I had been judged and condemned for my human actions. I didn't get a direct response that you can say that I heard the voice of God, but in spite of my fears, I continued to climb and put as much distance between myself and the lava flow.

"I really don't remember the exact minute that I knew that I was not condemned for all eternity, but I had a vision of my wife, Jana, and my child who had died some years back. It was with great sorrow and joy that I came to realize that I was not dead and that I was to continue my mission."

10

One of the elders spoke up, "This is very interesting, but how does it relate to our current state of being, and how can it help us to defend ourselves from the hordes of the general's armies if they are to come?"

"My point is," Jo-Eb continued, "if we are to persevere and grow, we need to understand the makeup of this man who fancies himself as the savior of his world and dictator of all mankind. The story is told to make it clear that with perseverance and determination that if you will come together as a single entity that you will be able to protect your way of life and ensure that your children and your future generations will not only exist but will persevere. So ask yourselves, am I here to toil all my life without being able to provide for my wife and family, or am I to take a stand and jointly forge a life that will make it better for not only myself and my family but also for my neighbor?"

His rendition of the story cemented their resolution to enjoin for the betterment of all concerned. He turned his attention to displaying his plans. "First," he stated, "I always give thanks to God for all of his goodness, and secondly, I ask him for his help and guidance. With that in mind, I will take a moment to give praises to God for his mercies. Anyone who wishes to join is welcome. If you do not wish to participate in this, don't be offended if I pray for you also." He knelt down on one knee and raised his hands toward the heavens. At first, only a few joined in, then shortly thereafter, it seemed the entire congregation joined in. "Thanks be to you, oh God, for your graciousness, and I present myself before you as your servant and request that you bless this endeavor." He continued to provide his praises and made mention as to how grateful he was that he was among a people who were of like mind. When he finished, he heard a loud "Amen!" from those gathered.

He was moved by the positive attitude of the group, and with their reassurance he continued, "I was once a free man to choose my own destination, yet now I am a prisoner to events I do not control. Even though I am temporarily held captive by my physical surroundings, I am still, in my heart, a free man. I choose to defend you and your way of life over my own freedom because I know that in a long run, it will benefit everyone."

"But," came an emphatic response from one of the elders, "we are not nation builders. We have no desire to expand beyond our current borders. Our desire is to live in peace, and we could do that no matter who the king is. He will live in his own world, and we in ours."

Jo-Eb responded, "You may not be a nation builder, but the general is. Do you really believe he will go about his conquest and not need replacements for his armies? Any able body—man, woman, and child—will be subject to his draft. Your sons will be his cannon fodder, and your daughters will be taken to bear more children for his cause. No, my friend, you cannot hide under a basket, for he will overturn it and take what he wants, and you will be helpless to protect yourselves." That seemed to be the straw that broke the camel's back.

It was the motivation that they needed to the cement the bound that brought the villages together. They now had a common interest in setting their own addenda for their lives. Each representative vowed to return to their towns and to serve each other in mutual protection against the onslaught of tyranny. Once this was complete, Jo-Eb reported back to Lady Jessica.

"The wheels are in motion," he reported. He gave a detailed account of the number of villages and the number of each person able to form a united front against any armies that would come their way.

"That's all well and good," the lady Jessica replied, "but they will not be strong enough to repel a well-trained, well-armed army such as the general has."

"That is all the more reason we must prepare them," Jo-Eb responded. "I have mapped out the routes that such a massive army will have to take in order to achieve a tactical advantage from the north and the west. A relatively small band of well-organized men can slow the advance and make it so costly that it will be virtually impossible to launch a battle from those directions."

"Yes," the lady continued "but eventually they will break through and proceed towards us."

"Exactly," he responded, "but we do not need to wait until they've broken through to engage. We simply have to have a plan of attack with a contingency to serve as a backup when things don't do as we've mapped out. Right now, we have the momentum, and if we continue to feed it, we will present a formidable front to deter action from those directions."

Lady Jessica considered this a good plan and decided to reinforce the villages with the arms and supplies available to shore up the small, emerging army of the villages. One thing she was worried about though was that the main thrust would more likely come from the southeast, given where their potential enemies were currently positioned.

"The main body will come from the southeast," Lady Jessica said, "and I really don't expect to see an all-out assault from those areas where you have selected."

"Yes," he responded, "but it will serve to keep open the lines of communications between us and the king's castle. I view that as a vital part of the operation. Now with your permission, I'll attempt to accomplish on our eastern and southern borders the same deterrent effect. I have studied the lay of the land in those areas and have determined that although there are some best routes, there are few restrictions on his ability to move his army across the area. Therefore, I propose that we formulate a battle plan that will slow him down the best we can, and that will cost him dearly for his efforts. We can build a great complex of walls and reinforce them here, but we will never be able to defend this without assistance from the locals."

As they were discussing the plan of action, a courier arrived from the castle. Mr. Barbosas had discovered and copied advanced plans for the weapon he identified as a catapult. It had the ability to hurl huge stones for several hundred yards and would present a devastating effect on an oncoming army. Even better, a smaller version of this weapon could be built and placed on wheels. Jo-Eb reflected that he was happy that Mr. Barbosas had continued to research the archives. They realized the potential right away, and the lady ordered to begin the construction. She would have three stationary catapults placed at each corner of the newly constructed wall. This would offer 360-degrees coverage. She also commissioned to have as many portable ones built to be placed in spots where an advancing army would have to thread through the valleys below. If handled correctly, assuming they had enough time to establish these weapons, the cost of advancement could help determine the final outcome of the battle once it ensued.

Once again after directing the placement she sent Jo-Eb to the south and east to determine how to best slow down the advancing armies. He found that he was most successful when he started with an opening that referred to Jessica of Dalliance. As she had previously stated, she had been a commander of a rebel faction before being taken prisoner by King Ruper, and her fame was still held in high esteem in these parts. What Jo-Eb thought would be a hard sell turned out to be relatively easy, as they had no love for the king and even less for the general. They had been ravished by his exploits in the past, and many of their sons and daughters had been hauled off to support his cause. With motivation as a background, he was able to attain maps of the various areas, and with the help of the rebel command, he was able to establish a cohesive offensive plan.

"You realize, of course, that no matter who comes across our land, be it the general or the king himself, we will do all in our power to thwart his encroachment on our lives. We've been in this fight for a long time, and we will continue to do so after you have long gone."

"Good," Jo-Eb replied. "That will make it easier to train you. You see, you have not encountered the full force of an army of twenty thousand well-armed seasoned troops, and if you are to survive, you will have to learn some new methods of defense."

They discussed the probabilities and the most-potential threat to be presented to them. He found that the use of his identification with the Lady of Dalliance was extremely helpful. They inquired of her well-being and expressed a desire to once again align themselves with her. They claimed that they knew that she had become an ardent supporter of the kingdom although not necessarily the king himself, and he replied that in this country under the current established government, the king and the kingdom were inseparable. This did not sit well with them, and they claimed that they would have to hear that from her mouth and not from a prisoner. He did not pursue the issue, as it was his business to formulate a formidable opposition and not discuss the issue of her allegiance.

As it turned out, the news from the front related that the campaign had not gone as smoothly as the general had expected, and the cost and losses of his men were much greater than expected. It seemed that the fighters of the territory were much more organized and equipped than it was first reported. The battles were won, in some cases just barely, but the cost was proving so much greater than anticipated that the king grew disheartened with the general's plans. He sent a second time for another legion to reinforce his current contingency and ordered the training of at least two more divisions in order to support this campaign. The days dragged on to weeks, and the weeks into autumn. With the onset of the winter, the king was considering a strategic withdrawal to resupply and return in the spring for a second attempt.

While all this was going on, the Lady of Dalliance was covering the southern region that she had been given as a trial area, and although she continued to preach the need for the people to be able to defend themselves, she also established and improved on the road networks. She presented to the people a new way of growing the crops and obtaining the water needed to supply the needs of each village. A network of aqueducts was being constructed to allow the rivers to accumulate water during the rainy season and preserve it into the long, hot summer months. Her plan was to widen and deepen the red river to ensure that huge pockets of water were trapped during the rainy seasons and provide a method of extracting the water as needed during the extreme dry seasons. She told them that the idea would take many years to develop, but if they would keep at it, in time, the entire region would be one lush farmland. To the farmers, the idea of longer, more fruitful crops provided a continuous incentive for the people. They were no longer rebels without a plan; they had become a common entity with a goal. She assured them that once their crops were accepted as beneficial to the kingdom that the king would be disposed to allow them to benefit themselves as long as they were being part of the link that allowed the kingdom to grow.

"That's a pretty idealistic viewpoint, isn't it?" Jo-Eb stated.

"Yes," was her reply, but we've got to start somewhere. It's my plan—should I live long enough—to see these people provide for the building of our nation even they don't see themselves as nation builders. It's my belief that someday, no matter who is in charge, that the leaders of the land will see the benefit of the people as being essential to their own well-being."

"Perhaps," he replied.

One day, the lady received a secret message via the secured route that had been established. The king had received her classified message and, at first, dismissed it as overreaction on her part but now was considering the ramifications of her concerns and had decided to be cautious in his involvement in the actual battles. Twice, it seemed that an area of danger had exposed him to possible capture and even death. He had managed to escape them, but now he was leery of what may have led up to those situations. He expressed his gratitude for her allegiance to the crown and promised that should he survive this, his future plans would give more credence to her point of view.

One day, the lady received a strange communication from the castle. It seemed that a small group of gypsies had traveled through the area and had asked about the man from the west. The captain of the guard has spoken to them and had not relayed the entire content of his talks, but it was reported that they asked several questions, sold their wears, and moved on. In his message, the captain relayed that he was leery of them, as they did not seem to be the normal gypsies. He couldn't put his finger on it, but it just didn't sit well with him. He stated that he was careful not to divulge any information about the whereabouts of Jo-Eb but just had that eerie feeling that something wasn't as it was reported to be. He sent a squad to follow them to see if he could find out more information.

    She called for Jo-Eb and relayed the story to him. She also reminded him of his word not to try to escape. He simply smiled and responded, "I'll keep my word. As long as I am a prisoner and working in your service, I will not attempt an escape." Some days later, she received another message that the squad trailing the gypsy band had followed them to the northern border about three hundred miles to a town where they seemed to be settling in for the winter. That being the case the group had returned with their report. She made no more mention of the situation but kept it in the back of her mind. She often told herself that you can never be too careful. On another occasion, Jo-Eb was instructed that a secret message had come directly to him. He kept quiet about it, as although he promised not to attempt an escape, he never promised to tell her everything he knew.

The message was from an unidentified source although he had no doubt from whom it had come. It simply said, "Hershel knows." Apparently, the gypsies were not all that they had passed themselves off as. The message had taken a long time to arrive, as it had been passed on by mouth through several townships. Since the people had grown a likeness for Jo-Eb because of his attitude of service to the people and not necessarily to the king, his name was a popular one, and the news had spread quickly even as far north as the Dakota area. The local people were only too glad to spread the word without notifying the king's court. Nothing, however, slipped past the lady Jessica's spies. The message no sooner left the lips of the messenger than she had Jo-Eb called to her tent.

"What secrets are you keeping from me?" Lady Jessica's voice was tart, and her face was flushed. "How is it that you can receive a message not sent directly to me first?"

"I kept no secret from you." Jo-Eb paused for a few seconds then continued, "I did not initiate any message nor did I know of its existence until this very minute. Besides, there are no secrets that can go past these gates either way without your knowledge. Would I have told you the message if you had not called me? No, I would not. On the other hand, I knew that any message would be reported in record time. I didn't have an opportunity to think about it before you summonsed me. No, I have kept no secret from you."

"Well." She seemed somewhat calmer now. "Then what does it mean?"

"It means exactly what it says, 'Hershel knows,' nothing more and nothing less."

"Well, who is this Hershel, and what does he know?" By this time, she had completely relaxed and was toying with him.

"I only know of one Hershel. I have been his friend for some time now, and I can only guess as much as you do. He knows I am alive. There was some doubt about it after they cave in. Now, apparently, he has received confirmation that I am, in fact, alive. I do not know where the message originated from. I suspect it's from our side of the divide. I don't know what, if anything, he plans on doing about it."

"Are you hopeful that he will attempt a rescue?"

"One can always hope, I suppose!" His answer seemed to amuse her.

"Yet you have promised not to attempt an escape. How will you reconcile this if he does attempt your rescue?"

"If you are trying to get me to say I will not go if rescued, you'd be asking me to lie. I will not attempt an escape, but if the circumstances warrant, I will make use of whatever legal means that I have to available to depart. I will not break my word, but here again, I am not fond of being a prisoner of your kingdom."

She did not reply; she simply waived her hand in dismissal, and he departed.

She wanted to give this situation some thought. On one hand, he was keeping his word, and on the other, she had to ask herself if his presence was worth the worry. If she returned him to the castle, at least he would be secured, and she wouldn't have the worry. On the other hand, he was a valuable asset and had given wise council on several occasions. Besides, the locals liked him. So now she had to ask herself, if I were to send him back, how will the provinces react? After all, she kept telling herself if the peasants did not like her decision, despite the fact that she enjoyed a certain popularity, she knew that not all village leaders would be unquestionably loyal to her and certainly not the king. After she thought on it a while, she decided that sending him back to the castle would be best for everyone.

After cementing her decision she called a council of the officers and included Jo-Eb. She explained what the circumstances were and that in the interest of his safekeeping, she was sending him back to the castle. She made it a special point that although he had kept his word and was well liked by the locals, it was her decision in the interest of continuity that he would be returned back to the castle. She thanked him for his service this far and made a special point to express that he in no way should be punished, for she admired his honesty and integrity. She then turned to the officers and spoke very softly and sternly, "This situation could blow up in our faces. If the people of the province feel that a friend has been taken away from them, they may be less likely to assist us. Keep that in mind I caution you to be cordial in what you say and the tone of voice that you use. As far as I am concerned, he is going on a mission and will be gone for a while. Spies are everywhere, and one wrong word or move on anyone's part can destabilize the situation. Jo-Eb has been honest with me, and I intend to see that he is treated with dignity and respect. Do I have any questions?" That last statement left no doubt that anyone caught upsetting the apple cart would wind up in sever trouble. After they left, she sat down and immediately issued a communique to the king. She explained why she had taken him out of the prison cell in the first place and that he had been extremely loyal to his word and gave no indication that he was to be considered a flight risk. Having accomplished that, she retired for the evening.

11

The next morning, Jo-Eb requested an audience with Lady Jessica. "I have given my word and will continue to abide by your wishes. My only request is that you allow me to address the people so as not to upset them. If I am simply sent away, it will undoubtedly upset some of them, and it could, as you stated yesterday, have a negative impact on their cooperation. I completely understand your stance on this situation and have no animosity towards your decision."

Lady Jessica paused for a minute then responded, "Okay, I'll call a meeting of the elders. It will be up to you to present yourself as sorrowful that you must leave, but when duty calls, you must go." He was in agreement both in voice and content. After all, it was his current situation that he had to be concerned about, not an ideological stance.

Later that day as he met with the elders, he relayed that his mission required complete secrecy and he did not know when or even if he would ever return. He enthusiastically endorsed the lady Jessica and requested that they align themselves with her as well as they had with him. "We don't know which way the wind blows or how hard it will. Yet," he said, "we've got to do our best to provide mutual protection of our lands so you can keep the wolves at bay." As he concluded his speech, they had a short social session. A couple of the elders approached him and relayed a message that if at any time and for any reason he had need of them, he could count on them for support. It made him feel good to hear that although he figured that such would never be the case. To that, he responded, "I have always attempted to leave things better than they when I arrived, and I only hope I have been able to accomplish that." With flare he mounted his horse and with his escorts headed north.

On the morning of the sixth day, they arrived at the castle area. As they crested the hill, it seemed strange that the gates were ajar and no sentries were posted on the wall. His escorts immediately drew their swords and started to gallop forward in a charge. "Wait," he commanded. "You may be riding into a trap. As a matter of fact, I'm sure of it."

The lieutenant in charge raised his sword in a halting manner, and he returned to Jo-Eb. "What do you know of this?" he inquired.

"Nothing," Jo-Eb responded. "I'm just as much in the dark as you are, but consider this: the castle was guarded by some one thousand soldiers and now gives no indication that anyone is on guard. What chance do you think you will have with only a hundred men?"

"Good point," the lieutenant responded. "Perhaps caution would trump valor in this case. What, if any, plan do you have?"

"Why don't you consider sending a squad with a flag of truce towards the castle? If they are not fired on, you may at least find some common ground to present negotiations. If they refuse to recognize the flag, you will definitely know that those in charge are completely hostile and have no intent of presenting themselves and that your death will be the obvious solution for their problem."

"Their problem?" the lieutenant replied. "How do you see it as their problem?"

"Well, for one thing, they must know that it is the castle of the most powerful king in a thousand miles in any direction. They also know that autumn is just around the corner, and in keeping with tradition, he will be returning soon, so they will not be able to hold their position for long. It would be an excellent bargaining chip if they are so inclined."

The lieutenant assigned a three-man party to provide a white flag and proceed toward the castle. In the meantime, he stationed his men to act in support of the patrol in the event they were fired upon. He was young, Jo-Eb observed, but he had a head on his shoulders. The party entered the main gate without any sign of an objection from those within. After a few minutes, a rider returned. "It's empty of all soldiers, and there is no sign of any hostile forces within," he reported. "The place is a mess with everything strewed about and no sign of life."

"Then we shall enter," the leader commanded as he placed his sword in the scabbard and started to proceed. "Wait," Jo-Eb announced. "Let's consider the possibility that the place actually has some adversaries hidden just awaiting for us to enter the gate. Once closed on us, there will be no possibility of escape, and it may actually spell our doom."

"Once again," the lieutenant responded, "wisdom seems to have trumped emotions. What do you have in mind?"

"Withdraw your men from the castle, turn about, and give the impression that you are heading away. You can station a few men just beyond the crest to see if any activity occurs within the castle. If they send out a scouting party, you can capture them and interrogate them to find out their strengths and weaknesses. With that knowledge, you can formulate a plan of action. The leader gave the command, and the riders returned from the castle. He made a grand display of unfurrowing the legion flag and turning about. They marched off in a column of twos while singing a troop song. Once they had disappeared over the hilltop, he had the majority of the troops to continue singing and marching for a short while until they were safely away. As suggested, he placed a small entourage of six men stationed in the rocks well hidden from the sight of any advancing force. Sure enough, not very long later, a group of three men crossed over the hill and started on the downward slope. Those stationed between the rocks quickly closed their escape route and pushed them toward the troops. The lieutenant had wisely fashioned them in a *V* formation, and very quickly, they were entrapped. "We can kill you," the young officer called out, "or you can surrender and live." At first, they formed a triangle of self-protection but very quickly realized that their situation was useless, so they threw their swords down.

"Smart move," the lieutenant called out. "Now come and enjoy a good meal with us and have some ale." The three didn't know what to make of that, but they humbly complied.

"Very shrewd." Jo-Eb observed. "Very shrewd indeed." They sat for the better part of an hour while they ate and drank.

While in conversation, the leader seemed to lighten up some and began to talk. His group had been part of a much-larger force that had conquered the castle and had left a couple of days back. His group of eleven had decided to stay and enjoy the provisions that were still available after the main force had taken control. He could only account for some three hundred defenders when they arrived and had no idea why it was so lightly defended. It was a costly mistake on the part of the captain of the guard to not have a more vigilant watch, and the ensuing battle was actually short lived. The lieutenant looked at Jo-Eb. "How much of this do you think is true?"

"Well…" Jo-Eb hesitated for a few seconds. "I'd say the ale has loosened his tongue some, but I'm not sure how much stock I'd put in his claims. Perhaps we can offer to send one of them back to the castle with an invitation to come out and depart as friends rather than to stay in there and face certain death. If he speaks truth, I suppose they will be willing to follow his lead. If not, we may have a battle on our hands."

"Friends?" the lieutenant replied. "I wouldn't treat them as friends."

"Neither would I, but I'd sure like to take them out in the open rather than have them ambush us within the castle walls."

"Once again, your wisdom shines through. We'll send forth the invitation and see what happens."

Several hours later with messengers being sent back and forth, a group of eight men came out and posted themselves before the main gate. Apparently, there had been quite a bit of bickering amongst them, and finally, the leader pronounced that they would trust the soldiers. "After all, he contended they have provided a lot of ale to us today and everything in here is gone. He can't be all bad." The lieutenant and his hundred men rode into the castle. He had the vagabonds bound and placed in the jail cells and assigned people to the wall for its defense and another crew to start the cleanup and to gather the dead. One thing seemed to be true: the bodies were starting to rot and gave credence to the statement that the battle had been at least five to seven days back. While they were completing their assigned tasks, Jo-Eb went to the library. He found it empty and was concerned about Mr. Barbosas and his family. After a short search, he determined through a series of encoded messages that Mr. Barbosas had retreated to the dungeon below where he and Barbara had been held. As he descended, he saw only one torch which dimly lit the corridors that led to the main door where he had been kept. "Mr. Barbosas" he called, "don't shoot. It's me Jo-Eb."

"As a wise man once said, 'Only fools rush in where wise men fear to tread,'" was the reply. Jo-Eb presented himself and Mr. Barbosas and his family met with the lieutenant in charge in the king's conference room.

Mr. Barbosas relayed how the events had unfolded where the general had ordered all but a bare minimum to report for the battle, as he needed replacement and didn't give a hoot or a hollower about the castle. After all, in the unlikely event that it was overrun, he had an army of more than twenty thousand seasoned troops and could always take it back. "When that happened," Mr. Barbosas said, "I took all of the books from the library that I could transfer and hid them. I have several good spots where they will remain safe if the marauders overtake us and go about destroying everything. As it turned out, it was a wise decision. I moved the family down to your old cell and set up some traps to dissuade any invaders from entering, then I kept as quiet as a mouse. We'd stored up several weeks' supplies. It's a good thing you dug that cave into the wall behind the drawers—it proved an excellent spot to store supplies." He kind of chuckled at that.

The lieutenant seemed somewhat dismayed. "I thought you'd promised not to attempt an escape," he stated.

"And my word is my bond," Jo-Eb replied, "but this is called contingency planning. While I was stationed in the king's corridor, I was bonded by my word not to attempt to escape. Once I was placed in the dungeons, I had no choice but to set up one of several scenarios that may be used. I presented you with my word that I would not attempt to escape while we were reroute to the castle, and I now extend that commitment to not attempt an escape as long as things stay as they are."

As it turned out, the only officer left to guard the castle was killed on the first day, and now only one sergeant and two corporals were left in charge. They seemed to be unsure of what to do next. The sergeant reported to the lieutenant and pledged his troops, as they are to follow the orders and complete their assignments with vigor.

"Good," the lieutenant responded. "Now we can proceed." After placing the confusion on the back burner, he laid out a plan. He assigned three troopers from his command to return to Lady Jessica and report the events. He further assigned the sergeant and the two corporals each a shift to oversee the guards. "Sergeant Overbie, you will serve a double duty as directly responsible to all shifts. The two corporals will report directly to you, and when I have officers call, you will attend the meetings."

"Sir," Sergeant Overbie replied, "I am a good soldier and well versed in directing troops in battle, but I have no experience in directing others in this situation."

"Don't worry," Lieutenant Donavan replied. "We have plenty of experience in running the administrative issues. Jo-Eb, as long as you are here and have the abilities to establish a reasonable defense, I trust you to keep the activities of the soldiers such that they will present a formidable defense if the need should arise."

Jo-Eb simply nodded his head and sat quietly.

Once the basics were laid out and assignments made, Lieutenant Donavan called for the servants to provide a luncheon and instructed Jo-Eb, Sergeant Overbie, and the one corporal who was not on watch to join him. "The way I figure it, Lady Jessica will send reinforcements but that will take about ten days for the round-trip. I've dispatched the three with orders to report directly to her, as I have an eerie feeling that there are spies within her camp. I don't expect a frontal attack as the group that initially invaded and ransacked the castle most probable won't return."

Jo-Eb in his usual soft spoken tone spoke up, "The peasants can be of great value if we offer assurances that we will guard them during their time of need. I figure that you could send out a small squad to inform them of the current state of being and simply ask them to be our eyes and ears."

Lieutenant Donavan was, at first, somewhat reserved about placing his trust in the peasants, but after giving it some thought, he relented and decided to have Jo-Eb to act as emissary. After all, he had done that for Lady Jessica and never gave cause to give her any concern. In fact, it seemed to be working quite well. That being the case he told Jo-Eb to select three men to accompany him and start out for the villages. This was right down Jo-Eb's alley, as he was a congenial person and truly cared about others.

Upon arrival at the first village, he was met with resistance from the locals. They had their pitchforks and Maddoxes along with a few rusty swords but looked to present a formidable-looking opposition. Jo-Eb simply slipped off his horse, sheathed his sword, and raised his right hand in the familiar four-finger V and stood silently for a moment. The crowd seemed to settle down somewhat, so he advanced while espousing a pleasant yet commanding voice. "We are here as representatives of the king. We have come to offer our services to ensure the safety of your village and protection of your families."

"Yea, right," came a response from the crowd. "Just how do intend to protect us with only four people?"

"Not true," was Jo-Eb's response. "As the representative of the king, we are here to assure you that the protection of the castle will be afforded you if and when you are attacked. All we ask in return—" He was rudely interrupted by a "Here it comes!" comment. He continued without paying attention to the disruption. "All we need from you is for you to keep your eyes and ears open and alert us when any movement by a potential advisory is noticed. We will require food and drink for our troops and will pay you a fair price for whatever we purchase."

With that, one shouted, "Are you the Jo-Eb from the far side of the divide?"

"Yes," he responded, "and I believe in the dignity of every one. I am aware of the past treatment and know that you are skeptical of anyone from the castle, but as long as I have a say in it, you will be treated fairly."

"That's good enough for me," was the response.

Having established a modicum of civility Jo-Eb motioned that the three that accompanied him unseat and proceed to the middle of the town. As it happened, he had been able to select the three who were to accompany him. Since they had gone with him during his visits in the south, they were accustomed to his ways. They led all the horses to the stable, gave the stable boy a pittance, and politely asked him to feed and water them. The boy reflected a big grin and a solid "Yes, sir." The word went through the village that these soldiers were not like the bullies that normally come through, and it set the stage for a mutual cooperation. Jo-Eb attended the conference of the elders and explained how he would like things to go. He had a plan for mutual communications and provided a horse that he had brought along for this to enable the messages to be sent faster. This had never been heard of before. A horse provided by the king's men to assist in dispatching messages. While talking, Jo-Eb mentioned that this is now their horse and can be used to help deliveries to the castle if they so desired. They were ecstatic at the thought and were happy that he had come by. They agreed to set up post at various entrances to the valley and keep him informed as things progressed. They offered to have him stay overnight as the hour was getting late, and he agreed to stay.

While there, he struck up a conversation with the local merchants and inquired about the nearest town and if they had any connections with them. The initial response was that they did not trust the people of the next village as they had many turf battles over the fertile lands that lay between the two. Sometimes they would sew the crops, and the hooligans from the other town would trod them down and destroy the entire crop. So, of course, there was bad blood between them. He didn't offer any solution to the problem, but having had that experience once before, he had some ideas of how to bring about reconciliation. The next morning after a hardy breakfast, they headed for the next village.

When he arrived, he found that his presence was already known. As it turns out, the town has its spies, and they had reported the events of yesterday. "I have never met you each personally, yet I feel that I know you," he started. "Since you have already been briefed on my mission, I'm supposing it will be an easier day than yesterday's hostile beginning."

The village elders nodded in recognition and without reservation. Apparently, his encounter of yesterday proved fruitful. So without hesitation, he inquired to see if the council would meet with him. Once again, he arranged to provide a horse for the town and offered to have the markets of the castle open for trade. They seemed to be a mild-mannered assembly up to the point where one of them mentioned the disputed ground where the two towns were constantly at odds.

After listening to their complaints, he very casually offered some possible agreements that could be forged between them. Perhaps they could plant every other year or jointly plant each one half of the land and rotate it as the crops were different and would not deplete the soil. Then, as in the Bible, they could let the land rest every seven years to replenish and nourish the ground. He did not offer to act as an intermediary, as he felt his mission was not to govern but to be helpful in establishing trust and mutual cooperation. The elders agreed to contact the other township and see what could be worked out. Again, since the hour was late, he stayed over the night, and after a huge breakfast the next morning, he headed yet for the next establishment.

His arrival at the third place was met with rocks and arrows. Fortunately, their anger displayed was more of a warning than an outright attack. Either that or they were very poor shots.

"We've experienced your promises before," came a voice from the crowd.

One of his escorts drew his sword, but Jo-Eb motioned for him to replace it into its scabbard. "We wish to speak to your representatives," was his reply. "We harbor no animosity towards you and only wish to enter into a conversation that can be beneficial to both of us."

A frail-looking skinny old man stepped out and shook his fist at Jo-Eb. "I am the only representative of the people, and my word is the law, and I say we don't want anything to do with you.

Jo-Eb replied, using the same analogy that he had used in the last village, "And so you will hide under your basket and hope no one will find you. I am not here to promise you peace and tranquility forever. I can only offer you that which I have, and it will be good only for as long as I have any say so in this matter."

"You are not the king," a woman shouted. "We have heard your stories and of your promises, but how does that make you any different than the others?"

"My word is my bond," he simply responded.

This seemed to cause some dissention among the group, and some mumbled, "Perhaps we should at least hear what he has to say." They withdrew some hundred yards and discussed just what they should do about this character. After a time, the old, skinny man returned and stated that they would listen to what he had to say. Jo-Eb dismounted and approached as his men looked on. He had instructed them to stay on their horses to enable them to strike if it became necessary.

"I come to you in piece," Jo-Eb started.

12

It seemed that his efforts paid off. A deal was struck with the local communities, and a feeling of mutual respect seemed to prevail. He reported his success to Lieutenant Donavan and was sure he had contributed to the security of the castle. The next day, a rider arrived from the northernmost township with a discouraging message. A large company of unknown origin had been reported moving south toward the castle. It was reported to be so large that it was assumed to be an army of many thousands. Lieutenant Donavan immediately sent a scouting party to ascertain its size, military strength, and to determine their possible intent.

After three days, only one scout returned. He reported that that most of the party had been captured and seemingly executed without reason or mercy and only he had escaped. As the youngest, least-inexperienced member of the party, he had been left to tend to the horses while the scouts simply walked into the camp.

Their objective, of course, was to establish a dialogue and determine what the intent of the opposing nation was. The young scout referred to them as a nation with a number so vast that it stretched completely across the wide valley below. Jo-Eb suggested that messengers be dispatched immediately to the king's army and Lady Jessica's party to inform them of the potential threat.

"We have no way to defend against an army that large," Lieutenant Donavan stated. "Perhaps we can meet them and surrender in honor."

To this, Mr. Barbosas replied, "They executed several scouts while under a white flag. Do you expect that they will be of a frame of mind to negotiate a peace?"

With a combination of fear and determination the order was given to prepare for an all-out invasion.

"We have no chance, you know," the lieutenant responded. "Our only hope will be that the king's army arrives in time to overcome the hordes of barbarians that are coming our way. I don't expect we'll get much help from there unless the king is still in charge."

Not knowing was predominant on everyone's mind. "Well, I'd not give up hope yet!" Barbara stated with determination in her voice. "We can launch attacks from two different directions, crippling their advancement, giving the lieutenant time to reinforce the walls and perhaps delay the main attack for several days. It's all about gaining time, and I know just the girl who can lead that issue."

Jo-Eb couldn't help but smile. Despite the overwhelming odds, she wasn't about to give up. As he had been in several situations where it seemed almost impossible, he simply raised his sword and responded, "Long live liberty."

For the next several days, small bands went out to harass the enemy in an attempt to delay the inevitable. Fortunately, the weather had been in their favor, and the rains were in their favor. With the mudslides and the fierce storms associated with this time of the year, the opposition was ground virtuously to a halt. It's one thing to move an army under these conditions but yet another to move an entire civilization each day. Their success was not met without cost though, and they lost almost thirty-nine good warriors during the skirmishes. The enemy was fierce and well skilled in warfare. It seemed that no matter what was accomplished, they were destined to overtake the castle. After seven grueling days, the enemy finally made their camp just the other side of a hill close to the large lake used for water for the castle. The day of reckoning, it seemed, had arrived. The defenders were by no means licked yet, as they were convinced that they could hold out several weeks against the onslaught. They had time to prepare and had brought in supplies of food, medicines, and weapons from throughout the lands. The townsfolk gladly furnished them with as much provisions as possible. Their motivation was twofold one. As long as the enemy was concentrating on the castle, they had time to evacuate their current locations. This seemed to be a prevalent way of addressing insurmountable odds. Many of the town's surrounding the castle area simply vanished. The second was to attempt to let the enemy know that they were simply peasants and had no part in a war between the two opposing factions. Their goal, of course, was survival.

The castle stood for over two weeks, and there was some talk that the enemy would be simply weary of war and move on to something that would be easier to conquer. In truth though, almost 30 percent of the defenders had been killed, and their strength diminished daily.

Then for no explicable reason, without warning, the tide seemed to change. One morning as he looked out over the horizon, Jo-Eb noticed a sudden change in the weather. "The clouds are gathering about, and the warriors are restless. I've got this eerie feeling that we're in for a severe turbulence. Look at that outline of the clouds. Lightning flashes continuously, and there is a deep-orange glow around the entire perimeter. I've never seen such a sight especially in the early morning. I don't know. I just have this feeling."

"Perhaps you're right, Jo-Eb," Barbara responded. "But I don't see any movement out there. It seems that ever since we've locked ourselves behind these walls, we've been isolated and have no way to know just what's going on in the other side of that crest. They might have simply left."

"Or," Jo-Eb responded, "they just might have gathered more forces and are waiting for the command."

"Well," she responded, "there's no sense in waiting here and guessing."

"Well," he drawled out the statement, "actually, we've been quite busy. Remember the tunnel we started? We've been continuing to dig for some time now, and we've broken through on the other side of that mound." He pointed at the largest noel just to the right center of their position. "It's only a peephole right now, but we've got plans to set up trapdoors so we can go in and out."

They just stood there, staring at the clouds for what seemed to be the longest time. "Well," she replied, "has anyone tried a direct approach? We wouldn't want them to get the idea that we're sleeping in here." She had a twinkle in her eye, and her voice left no doubt that she was formulating a plan of action.

"Well," he replied, "as we're deep in the autumn, we're not expecting a frontal assault anytime soon. Since we've not had any people coming from the surrounding towns in a couple of weeks, I suppose they, referring to the unknown enemy, are reinforcing their grip on the surrounding towns and won't let them come in here."

Once again, she frowned, then a slight smile could be noticed on the curves of her lips. "We'll be running out of water if we don't get that cistern working again.

But I've got an idea. Close to the spot where you come out on the other side of that hill"—she was referring to the now-completed tunnel—"there's a rather large lake. If we drill down some, we can come out below the surface. We can obtain water without their knowing about it."

"Very clever," he replied. "Actually, that won't take very long as we're only about four feet from the water level right now, and a long reed could touch it." He immediately retreated to the old cell and informed the foreman of the change in plans. Fortunately, they had a structural engineer in charge, and she immediately grasped the concept and went to work on the modifications. Juanna claimed to be a direct descendant of the Amazon queen from a faraway place called Congo. Jo-Eb looked it up in the old books available and had decided that her stories about the great land across the sea seemed to be in line with the records, such as they were, so he had no reason to doubt her tales of old. She could sit for hours and go on about how the Amazons had discovered and refined the art of construction. So far, her predictions had proven accurate, as she had declared that it would take three weeks and two days to tunnel through and they would wind up some three to four feet from the water's edge. Now with a new direction given, she started work on a trapdoor that would be set in place beneath the surface and would regulate the amount of water allowed in.

She told Jo-Eb that she'd have it finished in three days and the water would flow. Jo-Eb returned to the area where he supposed Barbara was still waiting. What he discovered that Barbara was nowhere to be found. He had no idea what she had in mind, but he was sure she'd be successful at it whatever it was.

He proceeded to check the progress on the walls. Juanna had taken the sod extracted from the tunnel and baked them into blocks of clay that formed reinforcement for the walls. Many portions of the walls had been destroyed during the first weeks of the aggression, and now they had a means to replace the broken parts. She had designed the boxes so that they were placed on a track and now had an assembly line set up. This afforded them the possibility of making over a hundred blocks each day, and as one container on line was emptied, it was returned on the oval track to be used again. Repairs were going along so well that they had completed the replacements and were now thickening the walls for additional stability. Another thing she had put in place was to take the broken stones and insert them into the mud while they were still curing, which made them even stronger.

With the placement of the walls being completed, the captain of the guard had ordered a maze constructed around the outside wall. The way he had it planned, it would funnel the enemy into smaller and smaller areas where they would be blocked by their own dead from retreating and smothered by hot lava-like liquids. The plan was to extend the outer walls into five tiers. Each successive wall would be higher than the preceding and would allow the defenders to always have the advantage of the higher elevation. "It won't be impregnable," The Captain would often say, "but they'll pay dearly for each foot of ground."

Jo-Eb looked out over the horizon again, and it seemed that the clouds had grown darker. The lightning was increasing now, and the thunder was like the roar of a thousand cannons. Even the orange sky had grown darker. "Well," he said to no one in particular, "at least we shouldn't have to worry about an attack."

A voice from behind, one he immediately recognized as Barbara, replied, "Yes now will be a great time to strike. They'll be hunkered down to wait it out, and a small contingency of twenty can wreak havoc on their camps."

"Excellent idea!" he responded. "Do you have anyone in mind to lead this expedition?"

She simply smiled and called to the captain of the guard, "Do you have that attack crew ready yet?" The captain responded with a simple wave in his usual approving manner and went back to inspecting the walls.

For the past month, Jo-Eb had been unofficially in charge, and all the actions had gone through him as the chief coordinator. The young officer who had escorted him back to the castle, in what seemed so long ago, had been killed in the first day of combat, and the captain of the guard was an inexperienced young man who immediately recognized his position and had turned over the command of defending the castle to Jo-Eb. He mentioned that if a relief column ever came that he'd have to take charge again. Jo-Eb told him that he'd not have any trouble, as he recognized his status as a prisoner. That being said, he was not about let the castle fall. He had too many friends behind these walls and would gladly accept the responsibility until the relief column arrived. In his mind, he did not believe the war general Jagaren would send reinforcements, as he apparently had no regard for the king's castle or the people confined therein.

By this time, the rain and the wind had become so fierce that he had little hope that the small attack force would be successful. *They're probably held up in a cave somewhere,* Jo-Eb thought to himself. The thunder was so loud that it was hard for him to even hear himself think, let alone to converse with anyone. *Too bad,* he thought. *It probably was a great idea but it won't happen in this weather.* He managed to return to the library. Since it was actually located below ground and in the center of the castle, the noise was less piercing, and by shouting, they could at least have a conversation. He spoke to the captain of the guard and directed that he reinforce the guard, as just as it was a good idea to launch an attack, the possibility existed that they might have the same idea. As it turned out later, it was a wise move, as some twenty-some odd aggressors had exactly the same idea that Barbara had and made the attempt to breach the walls. Due diligence had thwarted their plans, and twenty of the enemy were killed, and three captured.

As the rain let up and the skies cleared, he received reports that Barbara and her band had returned. She reported that there was no way of knowing exactly how successful they were, but she could account for at least sixty-five enemy killed, and she also brought back four who looked to have markings on their uniforms that would indicate that they had some type of leadership role. "We weren't able to set anything to fire, as the rain was so dense that nothing would stay lit for long. We did manage to stampede three corrals of horses though and destroy a dozen chariots. Unfortunately, we lost three of our own. They were caught in a mudslide, and although we spent some time looking for them, we had no luck. I thought now that the rain is letting up, some of us will go back to see if we can retrieve them. I wanted to deliver the four prisoners first though as I suspect that at least one of them"—she pointed to a frail-looking lanky man who was showing his age—"might be able to tell us something about their strength."

"I'm sure he could if he would," Jo-Eb replied, "but it's highly unlikely that he'll talk." As he said this, he gestured to the deep scars on the old man's face and arms. "He's a seasoned warrior, and most likely, he'd die before giving in to any torturer that we could inflict. Separate him from the others so he can't make any plans and give any orders."

With his permission she took a small group of five and went to see if they could retrieve those lost in the catastrophe.

The clouds separated, the sun peeked through the now-almost pure white sparse clouds, and some warmth returned to the day. The captain of the guard ordered half of the men to stand down, spread their clothing out to dry, get a good meal, and half of them were to return to duty, relieving half of those still watching the walls and instructed the remainder to get some rest. The plan was to return to the normal four-hour shifts, and by morning, they should be back to their normal rotations. He had set it up so that a new group would relieve a portion of those on guard every two hours and each crew would be allotted at least six hours of rest. It wasn't what he called optimal, but it's all he had to work with, and the soldiers didn't complain. Many of them had been with the war general on more than one campaign and quickly told the inexperienced young of how great this actually was. With the support of the seasoned veterans, the camp ran pretty much without undue tensions.

Jo-Eb commended the captain of the guard and instructed him to check on Joanna's progress, given the unruly weather they had experienced. He told him that he was going to retire for a couple of hours and was to be given a call when Barbara returned. Also, he gave the orders to that the enemy leader be fed, allowed to wash up, and be issued dry clothing. He figured that was all he could do for now, and since he'd not had a chance to change into dry clothing, he figured it was all he could do for now. Since he'd not had a chance to change, eat anything, and had been on his feet for twenty-some odd hours, he knew he had to retire or he'd be no good when decisions needed to be made.

He woke to a gentle shake of the shoulder and immediately sat up. "What's the word?" he asked.

"Barbara has returned with two of the bodies and reported that the third was nowhere to be found. She expects that he was probably buried under ten feet of mud, as the other two were on the edge of a cliff entombed under a couple feet of mud. They still had their spears sticking out of the ground, or they would have missed them all together. The third had been closer to the edge when the side gave way, so there was no way of confirming his status. Logic pointed to his immediate demise though."

"We'll accept that for now," was his reply. He didn't like loose ends and resolved to attempt to rescue the body if the situation presented itself. With that, he called for a conference in the king's meeting hall. He wanted Barbara, the captain of the guard, Joanna, and Mr. Barbosas there. The plan was to assess their situation and set a course for the next step.

After a ten-minute discussion gathering the facts, Jo-Eb announced that he was to bring in the leader captive. Since he had no idea if the men understood English or Spanish, he didn't know what to expect. With that, the man was brought in. Jo-Eb started with introductions of everyone in the room, had the chains removed, and offered the man a seat.

"I have no idea as to who you are or just what you and our comrades want, so I'm offering this opportunity to you to state your case."

For some time, the man just stared at him with a blank look on his face. After a bit, he responded, but Jo-Eb didn't understand his response, so he looked at the others to see if they comprehend what the man was saying. Each, in turn, returned a questioned look until he came to Mr. Barbosas. He, speaking for the assembly, told the man that he was in the land of the SW, a country ruled by King Richard, and that this was his castle. The man gestured toward Jo-Eb, and Mr. Barbosas translated. He is from a tribe of Ruskins who have migrated across the Bering Straits in the search for freedom from the czar. Through time, stories had been told of a king from the SW and his cruelty. With nothing else to go on, they decided to attack first and ask questions later. From what he had observed though, this king did not seem to be as bad as the rumors. Jo-Eb had to repress a laugh at that one. "Did you explain to him that I am not the king but just a captive much like him? Inform him that I am only temporarily in charge and subject to the captain of the guard."

The prisoner seemed to be confused by this. "How can a prisoner be in charge of the defense of the king's castle? That doesn't make sense."

Jo-Eb responded that it was a long story, but for now, they would take a break and have a meal. He told Mr. Barbosas to explain to him that if he would give his word not to attempt an escape that he would not chain him and move him to more comfortable quarters.

The prisoner then identified himself as Ivan of the cycle and asked what of his men. Jo-Eb said that they would have to remain in their cells for a while but they would be treated with the respect of warriors and made as comfortable as possible. This seemed to satisfy Ivan's concerns, and he agreed not to attempt an escape as long as the current situation remained. Jo-Eb considered him an honorable man, so he gave the orders. The captain of the guard agreed with his decision, so he ordered that the prisoners were to be allowed to clean up and be given clean dry clothing. Some of the younger guards murmured about prisoners being treated with respect, but the older and wiser warriors could see the sense behind it, so they passed on that the orders as given by the captain would be followed.

Jo-Eb called Ivan once more to the conference room. This time, he was all cleaned and stated that he was able to have the first good night's sleep in a long while. He asked about his people, and Jo-Eb invited him to attend while he checked on them. They went to the cell to find it had been cleaned and heated against the chill. Their clothing was clean and mended, and they reported that they had been treated well. One, the youngest, asked Ivan if they were going to be released soon, to which he replied, "I don't know. I honestly don't know what to think. These people are nothing like what we expected them to be."

As fate would have it, one of the guards was a descendant of the Ruskins and an avid researcher of his ancestry. He immediately offered his interpretation to Jo-Eb and was gladly welcomed. "Sir," the soldier explained, "I have studied the old language for years but never ever thought I'd have a chance to use it. As a matter of fact, I've slacked off the last couple of years and am grossly out of practice. I still understand what is said, but when I try to speak to them, they laugh at my accent. I told them that I would appreciate learning from them, so we've talked most of the night. In fact, I got so wrapped up in our conversation I forgot to leave when my shift was up. I hope that's okay with you."

Jo-Eb responded that he appreciated the fact that the guard was there and instructed the sergeant of the guard that this man would hence forth accompany him as an interpreter as long as the men were guest. The word *guest* was not lost on the guards, and their attitude reflected that they would go out of their way to accommodate them.

13

Jo-Eb instructed Provo, his new interpreter, to go and get some rest and, once rested, report back to him, as he wanted to learn as much as he could about the history of these people. With that, he returned to the conference room with Ivan. Mr. Barbosas was there now, so he was able to continue with what he had in mind. "First off," he started, "I've got to report that I am not the king of this land, and I cannot promise you how he will react when he returns. We've not had any word about his whereabouts or his circumstances in a couple of months. They may be held up for the winter in their battle area, or they might arrive here today. In either case, until that time comes, I will treat you and your people as my equal if you will agree to cease your attacks on the castle."

Ivan sat silent for a while, contemplating all that had transpired. After a bit, he replied in English, "We've been at war for a long time now, and although

I would not oppose a truce, I am but a centurion. I lead a contingency of the most-fearsome warriors in our clan. At one time, we were ten thousand strong, but over the years, we've lost over sixty percent of our former strength. While I would gladly embrace a peace treaty, I am only one of many and actually not very high up in the council. I don't know how well your proposal will be received."

Jo-Eb decided to go with his gut feelings and that he would trust that Ivan was an honorable man. He instructed the captain to arrange for a contingency to accompany him under a flag of truce. The captain gathered twelve of his most-experienced warriors, and they gathered at the main gate. With Jo-Eb and Ivan riding side by side, the other prisoners, unchained, were riding directly behind, and the twelve warriors selectively flanked them. Provo rode just to the right of Jo-Eb and carried the flag of truce. As they came to the crest of the hill, Jo-Eb motioned to Ivan to proceed and establish connectivity with the council. From the knoll, he could see the tents of his adversary. They were dispersed in twelve different camps, and all were arranged in such a manner that there was no doubt that they could provide an adequate mutual defense and, at the same time, launch a formidable offensive.

"Well," he said, more to himself then to anyone else, "at least we'll know what we're up against." They sat there for a long while, and it seemed that nothing was happening. All of a sudden, the entire army seemed to generate motion. While it looked chaotic at first, he soon realized that they were moving into an offensive position. He instructed Provo to bring the other captives forward and told them that they were free to return to their own clan. The corporal of the twelve asked why he'd let the enemy go since the next time they met them, it would be in battle.

Jo-Eb replied, "Do you think that six or more enemy warriors will really make a difference? At least they will live or die with their own kind."

The corporal nodded and ordered the release of the captives. "Say your good-byes now, as the next time you meet, it will most likely be at the end of a sword." Provo extended his hand to the youngest, the one he had established the most rapport with and offered him "Godspeed." He just knew that it would be the last time they would meet under friendly conditions and regretted the thought. The six turned toward their own camp and rode down the hill at a gallop.

As they neared the camp, those left on the crest observed a sudden shift in the movement of the camp. As rapidly as it had swung into action presenting a sure and definite threat, it settled into what seemed be a peaceful slumber. The fires that had been doused were being relit, and the camp seemed to go back into a rest mode.

"What do you make of that?" the corporal asked.

"I don't know," Jo-Eb responded, "but it seems we've lulled the beast to sleep for a short while anyway."

They sat there for the remainder of the morning. Finally, Jo-Eb instructed Provo to proceed down the hill to the edge of the first camp. His instructions were to inform them that Jo-Eb and his contingency would retire to a spot just beyond the crest and would wait their word in the shade of a tree grove. He stationed one guard at the top to keep an eye out for any movement and instructed that he be relieved every hour so as to keep the outlook fresh. *After all,* he thought, *we might be here for a long while, perhaps even days.* He sent one man back to the castle with the information that he had obtained up to this point and instructed that provisions for three days be provided. He also instructed the captain to send a dozen replacements each day for as long as this lasted. He was well aware of his precarious situation and that an attack could come at any minute. Yet in the back of his mind, he reasoned that the longer they sat in council, the longer the castle had to prepare for an onslaught if it were to come. Instead of cursing the unknown, he embraced it.

At the end of the third day, a small group of six men approached with instructions to have the leader of this party to present himself before the council. He immediately took Provo and started down the hill. "What if it's a trap?" Provo asked. "What if they intend to take you hostage or, worse yet, to kill you outright?"

"Well," he replied, "either I'll be a prisoner, or I'll be dead." Outwardly, he chuckled at the thought, but he couldn't settle the butterflies.

He hadn't had that feeling for a long time. He recalled the first time he felt it was when she placed his hands on her breast to wipe away the dirt on her blouse. Then quickly, he recalled his first meeting with Jana where she simply shook his hand when they first met. He thought it rather odd that this feeling would come back at a time when his life was in peril. Quickly, he placed those thoughts behind him as he proceeded to the encampment. They rode through the camps until they were directly in the center. He spotted a large tent decorated with the tribes of the twelve clans. He couldn't help being impressed. Everything was orderly and pressed clean. He was guided into the tent and instructed to sit and be comfortable. There were no chairs, so he was presented a blanket to sit on. Provo was left standing at his side and remained motionless.

As one of the elders started to speak, Jo-Eb raised his hand and stated, "Tell him that while I am honored to accept his hospitality, I cannot accept it until you have been accorded the same sign of respect."

"But," Provo objected, "it is not the way of these people to recognize a simple interpreter as an independent entity."

Jo-Eb simply replied, "In that case, our conversation is complete." He stood up, bowed slightly toward the council, and started for the flap.

"One moment." A thundering voice that Jo-Eb recognized as Ivan peeled through the tent. "While it is not our policy to provide for the needs of a servant, we will—out of respect for your custom—do so." Ivan motioned for a mat to be spread out for Provo.

"He is not simply an interpreter," Jo-Eb responded. "He is a fellow warrior."

"So be it!" was a response from one of the men standing in the corner. He was in the shadows, but Provo's expression indicated that he recognized the voice. It was the young man that he had spent so much time with and dreaded that they next meet at the end of a weapon. "Our ways are not your ways, but in this case, we will make an exception. Settlng this issue was paramount in Jo-Eb's mind, so they returned to their assigned spots. "We have been informed of your treatment of our people while they were your prisoners," the leader of the council said, "and we will extend the same courtesy to you while you are in our camp. Many of our leaders are dubious of your actions and intent, yet we find it intriguing that you have shown such civility toward a group identified as your enemy."

Jo-Eb simply stated, "We did not start this war and harbor no animosity toward your people. As long as I remain in charge, you will have nothing to fear from the inhabitance of the castle. While you might be able to conquer the castle and the inhabitance with your mighty army, ask yourself at what cost? Ask yourself—would a victory that cost half of your army be worth the price? A price you can ill afford especially since you can maintain your freedom and your strength and will be enabled to react when faced with a real threat to your families. I have conveyed to Ivan that we do not harbor any ideas of attempting to conquer you or subjugate you to slavery nor impose our will on you in any way. I am not the king of this land, but I have reason to believe that the king would not perceive you as a threat to his kingdom unless you continue to proceed in an aggressive manner."

"Yet we've heard the stories of your conquest." It was a low, steady voice, but it left no doubt in his mind that it was both from a renowned leader and a female. "Stories reflect both the good and the bad side of people."

He replied, "We have no wish to kill your young men nor to see ours die because of a story."

"Yet you have stated that you are not the leader of these people but simply a prisoner of the king yourself."

"True," he responded, "yet I've found him to be both an honorable man and a man concerned with his subjects. Should he return today, given the circumstances as they are, I have no doubt that he would launch an all-out attack. He commands an army perhaps four times your entire complement, and while I'm sure some of you would initially escape his wrath, I'm just as sure that his tenacity would follow you back across the Bering

Straits. I don't believe him to be a mad man, but I have no doubt that even if a remnant of you prevailed, the cost to your way of life would be devastating. No, I cannot guarantee you a peaceful acceptance on his part, but I do believe as long as he is in charge that sanity will prevail."

The silence was deafening. Not even one stirred or even crossed their legs. After what seemed an interminable absence of time, she replied, "Go now, and we will decide." Without so much as a word, Jo-Eb and Prove raised and left the tent. As they proceeded up the hill, Provo stated with some confidence that he was sure that a bargain could be struck. He hoped so, as he didn't cherish the thought of meeting his newfound friend at the end of a stick. "We'll see," Jo-Eb simply replied. "We'll see."

That evening, he opted to return to the castle but left the observers in place. He made sure that each man was fed well and had rested well before he returned. Upon his return, he immediately called for a conference to determine how things were coming along. He was interested in the defenses and especially the water project. While he was gone, a message had been received from Lady Jessica, stating that it was apparent that the war general had been killed in battle. The thing that gave her concern was the fact that the report that the wound had been inflicted from the back. She feared that if it was the action of one of the lieutenants that the king was now even in greater jeopardy than he had been before. Her news was weeks old, and she had no updates since that last message. He immediately dispatched a reply to let her know what they were up against at the castle. For a while, things seemed to go from bad to worse. The Amazon had completed the water box, and fresh water was flowing, but then they ran into a block. There had been a slight tremor felt on his second day on the hill, and the ground below shifted and caused a chasm directly in the center of the cave. It quickly filled with brine water, and now she was now conducting work around to restore the flow. It seemed that every time she was able to gain control of the situation, another cave-in would completely damage her structure. The area where the meat was stored had caved in, and the area that had been used for years to store fresh meat and vegetables because of its constant cool temperature had been breached, and most of the meat had spoiled. By the time it was discovered, many of the residents were sick, and dysentery was rampant. Fortunately, Mr. Barbosas had maintained the medical information of the past in chronological order and was able to identify the cause and the cure. They did lose several people, however, people who they could scarcely afford to lose. Although some might question his decision to retire for the evening, he knew that rest is as important as food.

He arose the following morning to be greeted by a blanket of snow. It was deep and very wet, indicating that although they had encountered a severe storm the night before, the temperature was such that it was very wet and made travel almost impossible. Mr. Barbosas reported that nothing like this had ever been recorded in these parts and the castle wasn't prepared for such a contingency. Just as he remarked that we should wait a while as things couldn't get much worse, the ground shook so violently that some of the walls of the inner court cracked and part of the outer wall crumbled into an opening in the earth. It created a chasm over ten feet wide and no telling how deep. Far below, there seemed to be a rain of fire flowing, and everything that had dropped into it immediately exploded. The smoke began to bellow out of the opening with a choking result from the sulfur smell, and confusion seemed to be the order of the day.

Jo-Eb called for a meeting in the conference room only to discover that it presented its own challenge. A huge hole had developed almost directly in the center of the room. "Well," he commented, "if the sulfur doesn't choke us to death, at least we won't have to worry about heat this winter." About that time, the earth belched again, and the hole expanded to swallow the conference table. He shook his head in exasperation and stated, "The king won't like that. It's his favorite table and chair."

"Perhaps we might see if we find a safer place to meet," Mr. Barbosas stated.

"The wisdom of the ages," Jo-Eb replied.

"Any suggestions?"

"The south side doesn't seem to be damaged much."

"Good, we'll move to the south side and hope it doesn't follow."

The room wasn't a grandiose as the main conference room but resounded with a sense of majesty. "What is this place?" Jo-Eb inquired.

"The main conference room of King Turbin, King Rogers's grandfather. That man wanted a meeting room off the beaten path where he could set in conference and not be disturbed. King Ruper moved into the new section when he took over, and King Rogers himself declared this to a shrine area to honor his grandfather. It seems we're back where we were fifty-some odd years ago but"—Mr. Barbosas paused reflectively—"those weren't such bad days when you recall them, especially in view of what we are now facing."

Jo-Eb replied, "Okay then let's get to work, first where are we?"

"Well, the good news is the fresh snow can be captured and will melt into fresh water if we don't contaminate it. We've stopped the sickness from the spoiled meat, but that poses another problem. We don't have much left to feed the people with. The reports from the scouts indicate that the Ruskins have been hit just as hard as we have. That being the case they won't be thinking attack for some while at least. Oh, and we've received another message from Lady Jessica. It seems her fears were founded, and the war general was killed by his number one lieutenant."

"That can't be good news," Jo-Eb responded.

"At least with the war general, you knew where you stood. Now with his number one in charge, I wonder just how safe the king really is. But enough for that for now, we've still got a greater part of the winter before us and not enough provisions or manpower to sustain ourselves. Perhaps we can get some small groups to forge some vegetables and get some meat. I'm sure the villages will be looking as we are and the Ruskins will be requiring food."

"Might I suggest?" came a voice Jo-Eb hadn't heard much of lately but was as welcome to his ears as any. "Whatever we acquire, we share with the locals and the Ruskins. It will put us in the short end of the stick for a while, but the dividends will pay off in a long run."

"Barbara's right as usual," he replied. "We will divide whatever we obtain into three groups with a third going to each. It will reinforce our position with the locals and give the Ruskins yet another reason not to attack us. A little food can go a long way towards ensuring our survivability." So he appointed the captain of the guard to send out patrols to acquire food. They split up into four groups of twelve each. The captain ordered two groups in reserve to go out whenever a group would return. He figured that way they could canvass the entire southern region for a distance of fifty miles and was certain they would find food. In his youth, he had traveled that track of land, so he made out maps by memory to ensure all areas were researched without wasting time in a lot of overlap and redundant coverage.

The first day wasn't very successful, but they did manage to acquire some venison and a couple of bushels of barriers. As planned, they split it into three sections, and Jo-Eb sent Provo with two slayed deer and a bushel of fruits to the Ruskins. Provo was to deliver it to the main council with the promise of more as they came across it. The second day went much better and enabled them to provide more rations and a lot of goodwill. He had the meat divided equally for the nearest villages and had them delivered. The townspeople were so astounded that some of the women broke out and cried. No one had ever brought any food to them in their times of need. One village responded to the gesture with an offer of dried fruits and nuts. Jo-Eb quickly suggested that they share it with their neighboring villages and also that they take some to the Ruskins. The locals didn't trust the Ruskins, so they declined. Jo-Eb then took a part of what they received from the villages and presented it to the Ruskins. He told Provo to be sure that they understood that the fruits and nuts came from the local villages.

Jo-Eb stated that "Perhaps we can turn this catastrophe into an advantage."

"Maybe," came a skeptical reply. This was offered by one of the young privates.

"Well, at least we've followed the commandments of God by attending to those in need. It's up to Him to take care of the rest." Jo-Eb hadn't thought of it in terms of his beliefs or convictions, but now that the young man mentioned it, it only made sense. He was glad that the private felt at ease enough to make a comment.

"Take the lemons that you've been given and make lemonade." Her voice was as clear and crisp as if she was standing before him. At first, it was his aunt Martha, then later, Jana repeated the same phrase. A tear swelled up in his eye as he remembered their voices. There before him was the two women that he had loved so dearly. They were worlds apart, yet they stood directly in front of him. Contemplating that thought he closed his eyes to rest for the night.

14

Sometimes dreams are a funny thing. They can bring joy and sorrow simultaneously. Often they lap over and confuse the sleeper as to who the good guy is and who is actually the scoundrel. Jo-Eb was having one such dream where he kept seeing Jana siding up to the witch, remembering his love for her and the witch kicking her so fiercely while she was pregnant. When he woke, he was lying in a pool of sweat. His body was shivering from the cold, as they had no fire in his sleeping room. He sat there for quite some time, trying to figure out where he was and how he'd gotten there. It didn't make much sense at first, as he could only see a dim flicker from the torch on the wall in the hall. He sat there for the longest time just staring at the flickering lights. It didn't make sense, and he couldn't put it all together. "Why," he kept asking himself, "Why would I have a dream that kept switching Jana and that witch?"

After a bit, he just lay back under the covers and fell back into a restless sleep.

The next morning, he awoke with a fresh vision in his mind. His vision was of providing support to the locals and especially their children. Up to this point, he had been concentrating on making contact with the leaders. Although this had proved somewhat successful, his new drive directed him to place the welfare of the children foremost in his mind. He knew that although his child had not survived the cruelty of this world that many others were born mostly without stature and even adequate provisions for survival to see them through for another day. Even before deciding to go to the mess hall, he took pen to paper and started jotting ideas. While standing in the line, he saw Provo and struck up a conversation. He explained about his dream and inquired if he might have any thoughts on it. Provo immediately responded that he had been in contact with Ezra. Ezra, of course, turned out to be the young man that Provo had befriended. As it turned out, Ezra was a direct descendant of the leaders of Tabasha tribe and held the astute position in the writing and directing of the laws. He and Ezra had formulated a close relationship, and Ezra had expressed his feelings and desires to teach the young. His insistence on following the letter of the law had been instrumental in convincing the council that they should hold off on an assault. After the great shaking of the land and a group showing up with provisions, the attitude of hostility dimmed, and some were even discussing trade.

When Provo approached Ezra about shifting his concerns from the adults to the children, the word spread swiftly through the camps. Some took to it right away, saying that anyone interested in the welfare of the children must be—by his very nature—a kind, gentle, and wise man. Some, however, were suspicious and stated that it was a ploy to pull away the youth from the loyalty of the Ruskin nation and turn them against the clans. Fortunately, Ezra's influence and insistence on teaching the young of the laws of the nation swayed most of the people, so there was no desire for war.

On the third day of the new hunt, the scouts reported back that a large herd of deer had been spotted, and a large section of hunters would be required to cull them. Jo-Eb saw an opportunity for a cooperative venture and instructed Provo to offer the Ruskins an opportunity to join in the hunt. The action would afford a joint venture and reinforce the trust of both people. He further sent news to the villages, requesting that they furnish tanners and skinners to join. The hunt lasted several days, and with the knowledge attained from the Ruskins, they were able to cull the herd without endangering it into extinction. The Ruskins offered to provide the skinners and tanners, as they had several who were experts in the arts. Jo-Eb explained that although they could furnish the experts, in his mind, it was imperative to foster a greater trust among the various factions to expand relationships and enhance trust. At one such meeting, he called for a feast and requested the councils of the Ruskins, the elders of the local three towns, and a contingency from the castle to meet. He had plans to propose an alliance of a more-permanent nature. The event was to be held on the knoll of the hill where he first established his outpost during their initial meeting. Since he sensed a certain amount of distrust, he arranged for the feast to be held in the open so those who still held distrust from either side would not feel they were being roped in.

The theme was established that each representative faction could exchange the knowledge of the other and perhaps reinforce the idea of the mutual trust arrangements to transport children into each other's camps and towns so the young ones could get a flavor for the history and way of life of their new neighbors. To relieve the tension, for those leery of what might be planned to kidnap the children, a series of tours was set up, and an equal number of children were escorted by their guards to the other's habitat. Games were set up, and refreshments were passed out to all. What was scheduled as an all-day event actually went on for several days with only a few hostile encounters that were perpetuated by too much ale and some boasting of the past, mostly by the warriors. Some of the fighting that ensued actually was between the different Ruskin camps. In the end though, except for those who had been hurt in the scrapes, everyone had a good time. Jo-Eb ensured that the members of the castle all had a chance to participate in the festivities, yet he still maintained a guard against any unforeseen events. After a week of celebration, all figured that the cultural exchange had proved fruitful.

On the last day of the event, a courier arrived, bearing a message from Lady Jessica. Her camp was under siege, and she might be driven from her stronghold. Despite all her preparations, the renegade army of the new general proved to be a much-larger force than she had anticipated, and she had no idea as to the current state of the king. Jo-Eb called his lieutenant in to conference and even included representatives from the locals and the Ruskin camps. He explained his current situation and informed them that he was leading a relief force in an attempt to save Lady Jessica and whatever contingency remained of her loyal subjects. He asked the townspeople if they would provide provisions for the campaign. At first, they were hesitant, as they knew that if he did not prevail, they would be subject to severe repercussions. He stated that although he had no right to ask for support from the Ruskins that they, at least, honor their word not to attack the castle while he was gone and even offered that they might ready themselves to move on short notice were he to be killed or captured. "Although I don't hold with kingdoms and czars, this is the world in which we live, and your main interest needs to be in the perseveration of your clans and your children."

To his surprise, the older lady who had questioned him on the first encounter stood up and stated, "We have been aware of your status from the start, and the council has voted unanimously to provide direct military support. We realize that this is not our own land, but we would like it to be. We will provide one thousand troops from each of the twelve clans. We will coordinate our efforts with your troops, and though they be few in numbers, we will accept your leadership." As abruptly as she had stood up, she sat back down as each of the twelve tribe members stood and raised their flags in a show of unison.

In an instant, he had an army of twelve thousand seasoned veterans. He turned to the leaders of the three towns with a questioned look on his face. "We too have come to realize the gravity of this situation, and you can count on our support." They responded. With that, the townspeople left to start preparing for their part in the mission. Jo-Eb motioned for the warrior leaders to accompany him to the library since the main conference room was still being repaired from the devastating quake of a few weeks ago. That horror was now just mainly a bad memory, as repairs were progressing nicely. He laid out a map of the area and presented his plan in a general sense. Although he set the objective, he asked the Ruskins to come up with a battle plan, as they provided the bulk of the actual fighting force and already knew the strengths and weaknesses of their comrades. As he explained to the captain of the guard, it just didn't make any sense to reinvent the wheel when they already had a well-oiled machine. The only reservations he had was that when the final thrust to break the backs of the aggressors happened, he and his people would be allowed to lead the charge. His reasoning was that when the time came, the defenders within the walls would not know of his alliance, and many might die before he could get the word to the besieged fort. He couldn't send word ahead, as he had no way of knowing if it would be intercepted, and didn't want to tip his hand any sooner than necessary.

They conducted a forced march for three days, arriving at what seemed to be a devastated scenery. Smoke bellowed from the wooden buildings, and bodies seemed to be stacked by sevens. They had encountered a few skirmishes along the way but, to date, had encountered very little resistance. Jo-Eb had an eerie feeling that things were not as they seemed and called for the Ruskin leaders to get their opinion as to just what was happening. They seemed a bit befuddled, as they were used to head-on competition, and the present situation gave cause for concern.

Jo-Eb ordered a quarter of the forces to flank right and left and a third quarter to guard the rear.

Something kept gnawing at him that made him recall some conversations that had been reported to him when he first accompanied Lady Jessica to the new fortress to be established. It had been reported that the war general's first lieutenant kept insisting on a partial frontal assault as a ruse while most of the bulk of his forces were behind the enemy. With that as a possible premise, he instructed the reserve contingency to keep a sharp look on their rear positions and be prepared for a massive combat assault. With that knowledge, each of the chiefs maneuvered the family move that divided one half of their force to support a rear attack if it came. As the day progressed, they encountered only scattered resistance. In the late afternoon, Jo-Eb sent word to have a third of each faction stand down eat and rest. By this time, he was concerned that a night assault would be the order of the day. His instructions were to give the appearance that the army had bedded down for the night. The chiefs quickly caught on and followed the strategy as laid out.

All fell quiet for several hours. Then with the rising of the full moon, the assault on his position started. Wave after wave, the oppressors attempted to gain the upper elevation and, wave after wave, was repelled. Instead of charging after the assaulters, he ordered that they stand their ground, and just as he expected, the assault was resumed. Had they followed, they would have fallen into the trap, and the results would have been disastrous. Four succeeding attacks were launched against their position, and with daylight, they could observe bodies stretched as high as a horse's bridle lay throughout the land as far as the eye could see. He took stock of their losses and was surprised that the killed was only listed at a few hundred. It seemed that the aggressors were caught completely off guard by this strategy and suffered extensively heavy losses. They scoured the land for the remainder of the opposing army but found only abandoned campsites. One of the chiefs commented that they simply didn't have the stomach for a defeat in battle and had simply retreated to their winter quarters.

Jo-Eb was not convinced, as when they were sorting out the dead enemies, he found very few officers, and even those were junior commanders. "I'm sure they will not rest the remainder of the winter. The climate here is favorable for battle most of the year in this region." Just as he was saying that, an idea flashed across his mind. "The castle," he shouted. "They're after the castle." He immediately dispatched scouts to scout the hills for any signs of large troop movements. He instructed his chiefs to send a forward fighting force to protect their people and warn the villages of their impending doom.

Once that was accomplished, he took a small force and returned to the smoldering fort. He found a lot of dead people, but since they pretty much wore the same uniforms, it was impossible to tell friend from foe. Some wore the insignia of their command, so those were able to be identified. After a couple of hours of searching, he still had not encountered Lady Jessica, and his hopes were rising that perhaps she was still alive. He was sure if she had been captured, the new war general would have her immediately executed and her head raised high on a stake to demoralize the enemy and demonstrate his superiority. As he found no such display, he was hopeful that perhaps she had escaped.

He sent messages to the surrounding towns to see if he could ascertain their status and see if they might have any knowledge as to the lady's present condition. He gathered the stragglers from the defending force and made sure their wounds were tended to and that they were cleaned feed and were resting. The reports were that the fort held for three days, and on the fourth, a charge was launched that would rival the stories of the Alamo. This was a story that had been repeated over the centuries about the final stand of a small village church some eight thousand years ago. A story that served as a focal point that turned the tide of battle and where a couple of hundred heroic men stopped a vastly superior force long enough to allow the independent forces to raise an army that ultimately defeated the aggressors.

By the end of the day, he was receiving reports form villages where he had visited when he was here the first time. No one could give a report about Lady Jessica though. It was almost as if she had disappeared from the face of the earth. He knew that he still had a war to fight, and as much as he would have liked to, he could not continue to search for her. He framed a small contingency to rebuild the fort as best as they could to provide services to the locals and assist them in recovery. Also, he directed that they see if they could find any information on the lady. Once this task was set into place, he turned his steed north to catch up with the main body. He was sure now that the attack from the rear, as costly as it was had been, lunched to stop him and his forces from returning to the castle. They rode for two days without rest and finally caught up with the main body. The reports were that the enemy had, through an immense, superior force, taken the castle in less than a day. The Ruskins, however, were another matter. They were a formidable force even without the twelve thousand that had accompanied Jo-Eb. Also, they were used to open-field combat and had managed to inflict heavy casualties on their enemy.

Jo-Eb reported to the head of the council of the state the condition of the battle in the southern region. He did not know for certain, but with each passing day, he was sure that Lady Jessica had somehow escaped the initial invasion, and he was hoping that she was holed up in the mountain area of the red river canyon. He remembered her stories of how she had been a rebel leader in her younger days and how she and others had managed to elude a superior force at a spot by the name of Masada. It was named after a Bible story of thousands of years earlier when a small band of rebels had held off an entire army with just a few hundred fighters. Unlike the original story where the rebels all committed suicide before being captured, she and her group accepted enslavement, and some lived to tell the tale and reunited to fight again. She had been so severely injured that she was taken to the castle to recover and become the king's emissary. Now he was hoping that she had made it back to that place of refuge where she could once again fight tyranny. It was some weeks before he received word of her whereabouts and condition.

In the meantime, he had work to do. After conferring with the war council of the Ruskins, he determined that he needed to get into the castle to see if he could determine the fate of his friends. He had established a pretty fair relationship with Ivan, and he managed to find Provo and Ezra. Provo had lacerations on his legs but was mending nicely, and Ezra had been stuck in the side with a spear. He still managed to strike back at the aggressors and downed three before he was bashed on the head and lost consciousness. When he woke up, he was in a battlefield hospital and insisted that he be transported back to his main council along with Provo. Since he carried the stature of a leader, he was immediately tied to a horse and led back to his home base.

Jo-Eb relayed his plan to them to enter the castle through the tunnel. They managed without too much trouble to find the small entrance to the cave that he had started so long ago. He wasn't sure what they might run into on the other side, but the best he could figure it, this was his best shot. He gathered seven volunteers, mostly from the castle guards because they had a better insight on land inside the walls. They proceeded toward the opening.

When they finally found the original opening, it was just a pinprick, so there was a bit of work to do be done before they could enter. Under the cover of darkness with a good cloud covering, they managed to break through in short order without being detected. It was imperative that they remain as quiet as possible, as they had no way of knowing what they might meet on the far side at the end of the shaft. As they approached the end, they ran into an area that had been blocked either by accident or covered to hide its existence from the enemy. Quietly and carefully, they commenced digging until, at last, he spotted a glimmer of light. Slowly and very quietly, he approached what appeared to be a sleeping figure. As he reached out to cover the mouth, he was jerked down on top of a body.

"Shhh!" He heard a whispered command. "Don't move until I tell you to."

The remainder of the crew stood perfectly still. It was the Amazon, and she lay perfectly still for a bit.

Then without warning, she started sobbing loudly and thrashing her arms. Jo-Eb didn't know what she was doing, but as she jumped up, she threw her blanket over him and proceeded to pound on the cell walls. She screamed and carried on for some time like a wild woman, and Jo-Eb didn't know what he could do to help the situation, so he did nothing. After a bit, she came back, and with full composure, she whispered, "It's okay now. I do this every night, so they just leave me alone. I was expecting help eventually but never thought it would be so soon. Anyway, Barbara is in the next cell, but I haven't gotten a report on Mr. Barbosas and his family. Since they are the keepers of the archives, I expect that they will be okay. I've heard that the captain of the guard is in chains, but I don't know how reliable that is. They have three Ruskin chiefs in captivity, but I don't know their condition."

"Well," he responded, "I have some of the elite castle guard with me, so I'm trying to assess the damage and the strength of any of our people."

"I'm afraid," she answered, "that any of those loyal to our cause won't be of much help. They're all changed to the walls, have been severely beaten and undernourished. Barbara and I have been kept down here awaiting our fate. I don't know yet if he plans to stock us or just kill us and be done with it."

"Is there any way you can get the guard over there to bring in the key?"

"Of course I can! Watch!" The last part of the comment was so emphatic that whatever she had in mind wasn't going to be pleasant for the guard. He reclined to the shadows as she sweetly called to the guard. After a minute, he stood up wondering at her sweet voice.

"I've been craving a man for a while now. Could you help me?" Her voice was so seductive that the guard stumbled on himself hurrying to get the key. As he swung open the door, she grabbed him pulled him close and gasped. Now that his attention was solely on the girl, Jo-Eb simply clouted him on the head with the butt of his knife. "See," she said, "I told you so."

They exited the cell, and one of the warriors accompanying him simply walked up to the sleepy guard and smitten him on the head. They took both guards to the very rear cell, tied them up, and gagged them.

"Why not just kill them?" one of the team members inquired.

"Because we may be able to get some information from them that will help us later," Jo-Eb replied.

Barbara cautioned that the two new guards would be coming soon for the change of the shift. Jo-Eb selected one of his men that was approximately the same size as the guard who was sleeping, had him cover his face, and just grunt when the two replacements arrived.

"Hay, wake up in there," one of the replacements called out as he peeked through the cell bars of the door. The man just continued to sit there with his feet on the table and grunted. The ruse worked, and the two new men entered. They were immediately met with the brunt end of a knife and slumped to the floor without a whimper.

"Tie them up with the others," the corporal commanded as they were dragged into the back cell and secured.

Jo-Eb designated one man to return to the camp. "Get as many of the castle guards as you can. We'll meet in the old conference room and dispatch our forces from there. Tell the Ruskins we'll have the gate open in one hour."

They hugged the walls and stayed in the shadows as much as possible. They only met two guards on the way and quickly put them to sleep. When they reached the library, he sought out Mr. Barbosas.

He and his family, although they had been treated rather roughly, were in good shape. "Somehow I knew that you'd be here soon."

"That's what the Amazon said. I'm glad you had so much confidence in me."

They smiled as he guided them to the tunnel. Shortly thereafter, twenty new support troops showed up. They were instructed to be as quiet as a church mouse as they proceeded to the main gate.

He formed them in a column of twos and marched right up to the wall in the usual manner of a relief contingency. As they approached, one of the guards on duty asked what it was all about because the changing of the guard just took place not twenty minutes ago. The sergeant of the guard simply replied, "And I'm an officer?"

The guard on duty shrugged his shoulders and turned back to the guardhouse. Five men followed him and quickly subdued him along with his two comrades while the other seven proceeded to the tower where the gate wheel was located. One guard looked up briefly, very briefly, before he slipped into unconsciousness. The other two had been looking out at the signal lamp that had appeared on the horizon. They too were sent into slumber, and the new guard raised his lamp. The remainder of those in the relief column continued to proceed to the succeeding towers and similarly replaced those on duty. In short order, the main court was filled with Ruskins all being as quiet as possible. They stationed themselves at the barracks doors and waited to minimize any attempts to exit and sound the alarm.

15

Jo-Eb poked Marcus with the blade of his sword to arouse him from his sleep. Apparently, he and some others had quite a celebration the night before, so he rose up groggily, slowly rose up in the bed, and wrung his eyes. At first, he acted as if it were a joke that the others had played on him, then in a few seconds, he feared that his second in command had treated him the same way he had when he took over from Jagaren Lightning. "What is this?" he shouted in a shrill voice. "What's the meaning of this?"

It wasn't until the seconds passed that it finally dawned on him that this was a stranger in his midst. "Sergeant of the guard!" he called out, displaying fear and confusion.

"No sense calling for help," Jo-Eb stated. "We've completely captured the entire castle area without much of a fight. Now you are to be transferred to your cell until we get word from the king as to your future."

Marcus started to lunge for his sword but was met by the broad side of a sword that brought him to his knees. "Secure him and place him in the small dungeon on the second floor. That way we'll be able to keep a close eye on him."

The actual takeover went a lot smoother than he'd hoped for. The vast majority of the soldiers under Marcus's command held no allegiance to him and actually welcomed the release from his tyrannical command. Although they vastly outnumbered the intruders, their weapons had been secured, and their way was blocked so they couldn't get out of the barracks even if they had wanted to. Jo-Eb called for a meeting of the officers of the vanquished command and presented his terms. They could submit to his leadership in support of the king and the castle, spend their time in incarceration, or attempt to fight their way out and they would surely die. Every man to a T bent his right knee and swore alliance to the king. Jo-Eb then ordered them to be released to their units with instructions to prepare to fight for their king.

He really didn't know where the king was or even if he was still alive, but he figured that as long as the masses were convinced that they were being loyal to the king, it would be a smoother transition. He really wanted to find out what had happened to Lady Jessica but felt it was his obligation to stay and oversee any changes that might occur. As such, he dispatched a battalion of troops from the castle guard to go to the area where he figured Lady Jessica might be held up. He instructed them to present a message that he had formulated and to return word as soon as they had something to report. He also sent a platoon of massager's to the area where the king had last been reported to be. In this case, they were cautioned not to go directly to the encampment but to attempt to discern the circumstances that they might encounter before making themselves known.

Now that he had accomplished this portion of the mission, he turned to the reconstruction of the walls and reestablishing a trusting relationship with the Ruskins and the local townspeople. Jo-Eb made it a point to converge with the locals at least once a week, and in doing so, he further instilled the trust of the inhabitance of the castle along with the Ruskin community. They resided in this environment for about four months when he received word that the king was indeed still alive but had been wounded in a battle some months back. Here again, the circumstances reflected that his enemy had come from within and not those he had gone to do battle with. There were some in allegiance with Marcus and had attempted a cue. Although the rebellion had been put down and the traitors met their just punishment, it was at a grave cost to the king, and they had been winter quartered since that time. Although he took no sides on the matter, he was glad to hear that the king had survived and was mending well. He received reports from the battalion that had gone to meet with Lady Jessica that she, in fact, although slightly wounded, managed to hold her forces together until the relief column arrived.

"It seems the course of events over the past several months has turned out much better than expected," Jo-Eb commented to his lieutenants at a meeting of the general staff. "We've managed to establish a trust relationship with the Ruskins, and the local villagers are prospering under the newfound wealth established between the three entities. Now with the return of spring, we're looking forward to reestablishing closer communications with Lady Jessica and perhaps the king."

It had indeed been both a blessed and a hard winter. At one point, snow fell several inches a day for nineteen consecutive days, and drifts were as high as a horse's bridle. The Ruskins accepted it as a way of life and didn't let it slow them down much, but the local residents were baffled. Mr. Barbosas researched and found that never in the archives had such a winter been recorded in these parts. As miserable as it was, it actually was just a nuisance. The Ruskins showed the locals how to deal with it, and survival turned out to be a method of bringing the separate worlds closer together. In all this time, Jo-Eb and the few people who were originally with him concentrated on securing the land hopefully for the king's return.

One morning, he was awakened to shouts of joy and celebration. He had been informed that the king had recuperated and was returning to the castle, so he started to get the house in order for his return. As it turned out, the king arrived several days earlier than expected, and Jo-Eb wasn't actually ready. Things were still to be done, and accommodations needed to be finalized so that everything would go off without a hitch. He hastily dressed and proceeded to the courtyard. He ordered the main gates to be opened and greeted the king as any slave servant would do. The king, seeing the condition of the castle and the state of the defenders, immediately commended Jo-Eb for his part in the establishment and protection of his castle.

"From what I'm told," the king said while sitting on his throne and stroking his long red beard, "you have managed to not only save my lands while I was away but also made an alliance with invaders from the north without a great, devastating war. I'm also told that the three nearby villages are prospering like never before."

"For me, it was simple," Jo-Eb responded. "I am not charged with ruling a nation, only keeping it intact until the rightful owner returned. Since I have no ambitions to rule, I did not have to contend with political maneuvers."

The king was pleased and ordered a celebration to last for two weeks with everyone invited. "Now what of these barbarians, the Ruskins? I understand they were most helpful in getting us through the winter. It was a hard one even where I quartered. We have never seen this type of a winter and had to learn from scratch how to deal with it. Do you believe them to be trustworthy now that the winter is over?"

Jo-Eb couldn't help but smile to himself. "If it weren't for them, we'd probably lost most of our supplies, and the villages would have suffered greatly. From what I see and what I am told, they have a desire to settle in this land. If you can find it within yourself to acknowledge them as humans, they will gladly pledge themselves to you. I believe that would be helpful since I know from the reports that a large army that has pursued them thus far is coming to destroy them and, in so doing, will attempt to conquer your lands."

The king continued to stroke his beard and sat silent for a while. "Then it shall be," he commented. It was both an affirmation and a command. "We shall live in peace. Have a representative of their nation come to the council chambers, and we will cordon off a section of land that will be exclusively theirs."

"One last matter," Jo-Eb continued. "I know that it is not the place of a slave to expect equal treatment within your kingdom, but I speak boldly in asking for freedom of both myself and Barbara. We have sworn that we will not try to escape and will follow your dictates, but if you could find it in your heart, we have resolved to seek freedom for ourselves so we can continue on our journey."

The king just sat there for several minutes. Never in all recorded history had a slave or a subject of the king requested a release. What type of precedence would this set for future request of this nature? How would it impact the very fabric of his kingdom? Who would be next, and how could he maintain control if Lady Jessica, for instance, requested her freedom? Would this lead to a breaking up of the kingdom? After a bit, he came back with an answer. "No, I cannot release you from your current state of being. What I can do is to send you out as an emissary with full power to search lands that I am not familiar with and establish trade routes. Of course, you'll have to take Barbara with you, as she has it in her heart to find this New York City. That way, I can proudly point to my generosity as a benevolent king who recognizes and rewards faithfulness."

Jo-Eb bowed his head and took his leave. "It's good to be on the trail again," he related to Barbara.

"Yes," she responded, "while I must say I did enjoy the company, I never lost the desire to continue my journey." They traveled for the next couple of days with little fanfare and concentrated on their mission. Jo-Eb's, of course, never changed. He still had his original quest to find Flower if, at all, possible, but now his fresher objective was to reunite with his family. He had not had any word of them for a couple of years now and had no way of knowing what lay next. Originally, King Rogers had ordered a full regiment to accompany him on his journey, but he, in requesting an audience, put forth the idea that a small group consisting of five or six volunteers who wanted adventure would be a more-formidable force, as they would not pose a threat to the inhabitance of the foreign lands and could travel much faster. Besides, he stated he was well known back in his land, and the thought that an army was invading them wouldn't go well for either side. The king, recognizing his wisdom, condescended to his wishes, and he put out the word for a half-dozen volunteers. He was looking for men who had travel experience and a desire to learn new ways to accompany him. Provo immediately spoke up as Jo-Eb wished he would, Robert as the chief historian and recorder and four others joined the crew. He wasn't aware of it at the time, but Provo and Barbara had become quite close, and as they traveled, he found them closer together. One day out of the blue, Barbara said that she and Provo had been talking marriage and wanted to ask Jo-Eb if he would preside. This seemed to be an established practice now, so he didn't even consider bring up that he was not an ordained minister. So many families had been started through this type of union he was only too glad to be asked to be a part of it. "What of your desires to go to New York while Provo is on assignment with me?"

"Not a problem," she responded. "I don't even know why I wanted to go to a strange place and become a stranger in a strange land. No, my place will be with

Provo." With that, as the evening drew nigh, he conducted the ceremony with the other five as witnesses, and the couple was set up in a camp away from the main group.

After two weeks of traveling northeast, they were confronted with a large territory that had been identified in the old scribes as the Ozark mountains. Although they did not rival the Rockies, it seemed that since they were last recorded, the tops were much higher than the old books indicated. On the few occasions when they met others, it seemed that they were most hostile and had absolutely no interest in converging except to steal what others had and take slaves and women for their own pleasures when they could. Fortunately, they never posed much of a threat to Jo-Eb and his group, as they were all experienced fighters and had established a close-knit method of common defense. The fact that the opposition never proved to be more than six or seven strong also lent to their ability to protect themselves. On one occasion, one of the warriors was hurt with a slash to the right arm, but that was easily mended, and since he stated that he was left-handed, it wouldn't pose a problem. They all had a good laugh at that, so the mission continued.

They happened upon a section identified in the old scribes as Merrimac caverns. No one knew exactly where they started or where they ended, and as a matter of fact, there were no records of how deep they went into the earth or what was to be found there. There were just a few references to the area, and it seemed that no one, no one of any historical value, had searched these caverns for centuries. One thing that came to light was that the deeper they went, the more light seemed to be coming from whatever was ahead. There were a few areas where they saw signs of some long-ago troop who had stopped or even perhaps perished there. As they rounded a narrow cliff, they spotted the source of the light. A light volcanic ash lay a few inches thick, and they had no way of knowing exactly what was underfoot. To test the depth they took long staffs and poked the surface to ensure they were not stepping into an abyss. Just as they were discussing whether to continue on or go back, they heard noises that sounded like conversation close at hand. Jo-Eb slowly advanced toward the source of the noise and found a small group of about twelve, mostly women and children huddled together. Two teenage boys stood in front of the group with staffs at the ready to ward off any invasion. Jo-Eb started slowly and, in as friendly a voice as he could muster, asked which tribe they were with. The frightened group didn't reply but stood their ground. So he tried again, this time in Ruskin and then English. The English brought about some sign of recognition, so he continued, "We are travelers in this strange land seeking the great river once named the Mississippi." There was some conversation amongst them for a minute, then one of the older ladies stepped forward. "We do not know of this river that you speak of. Our numbers once in the hundreds are now simply down to what you are seeing here."

"We mean you no harm," he replied. "We are simply traveling through and were looking for a way to the other side of the mountains to the east. On the surface, we've met with quite a bit of opposition and thought if we could travel through these caverns, perhaps we could avoid further battles."

"I know these lands and the caverns within the earth, and I can tell you there is no way to go to the other side except above ground."

"Have you ever followed the river?" he questioned.

"No, that would be foolish, as it would lead further into the bowls of the earth, and you would become hopelessly loss. No"—she paused for a slight period then continued—"I'm afraid you'll have to travel above the caverns to get where you want to go."

Noticing the majority of them was extremely young with only two teenage boys and two female adults, Jo-Eb offered help if he could. They had plenty of food to spare and would be happy to help if anyone needed healing assistance. At first, they were reluctant to accept anything, and then Jo-Eb remembered the old candy trick and presented some to the lady "for the children," he stated. Once again, as always happened, the candy did the trick, and in short order, the children were enjoying their newfound treasure, and the two adult women were divining up some of the grub he had to offer. "What are your plans?" he asked while they were enjoying a makeshift lunch.

"What?" the lady replied. "Well, we're trying to stay alive, and we live here, as we can't fight off the predators above ground, and we have no way of obtaining help."

"Well, you've got it now. That is if you want to accompany us. We can get you to a friendlier environment where your young will have the opportunity to thrive. I promise you we will do all in our power to protect you and the remains of your clan."

The two women and the two boys spoke for a minute then stated that it seemed to be the only way and would give them the best chance of survival. With the protection of the children being paramount, the newly formed alliance gathered their belongings, such as they were, and started back up toward the entrance of the cave.

As they reached the surface, they once again heard a commotion from outside the mouth. Jo-Eb cautioned all to be quiet while he and one other of the warriors went forward. As they exited the cave, they found three dead men laying close to the cave, and two who were wounded but not dead yet. They cautiously approached the area where they noticed yet another group just huddling around a body. Just as they were about to strike with their clubs, Jo-Eb charged with his sword drawn and screamed furiously, turning the aggressors into a disorganized, frightened group of individuals with no plan for defense. His companion downed two of them with his arrows and quickly wounded a third who hobbled off into the brush.

Jo-Eb, noting this was a small young group, decided to down the last two with the broadside of the sword. That way, he could perhaps get some information off them. "Can you get that wounded one for me?" he asked his companion. In no time flat, the wounded man was being dragged back into the area. Jo-Eb called for the group to exit the cave and gather the wounded and the prisoners into one area. He set out a post on both of the adjoining hills to preclude anyone from sneaking up on them and started with mending the wounds of this small band.

Once again, his instincts paid off. Of the three wounded men who had been left to die by their attackers and the one who was being attacked at the time he thwarted their advance, all were of relationship with his newfound family. He concluded that they wouldn't be able to travel in their condition, so he directed that all would go back into the cave and reside there until the wounded were well enough to travel. He reckoned that the time spent in mending would pay off in the end, as their strength would be almost doubled. Besides, the two older women recognized the group and knew them to be members of their once-proud clan. They stayed there for almost a week, and that gave the hunters an opportunity to collect some more venison. It was full summer now, and the days were hot. Within the cave the temperature held at a steady comfortable pace. At the start of the second week, the older man who was almost pulverized by the aggressors proclaimed that they were ready to travel. Jo-Eb recognized him as the spokesperson for the small clan and, out of respect, chatted with him as to their intentions. He promised that he and his small group would furnish shelter and security for them if they were to continue on the journey with him. He explained that he was headed back to his land where he was hoping to find his family and settle down there. If they were of a mind to they were welcome to accompany him. So it was decided. They would band together for a time, and when the situation presented itself, they would split.

Having made an agreement, they started early the next morning east toward the great waterway. His new companions had ventured several days east on one or two occasions, looking for food and perhaps some security for their small, diminishing clan, but after a week, they were back to uncharted territory. Travel was slow because the very young were not able to continue at the pace that Jo-Eb and his explorers were used to traveling, but he replied to one of them when they inquired that it was better to look after the needs of these strangers than to continue at breakneck speed not knowing where they would wind up.

As they reached a summit, once again, they looked out over the terrain. A fairly large settlement that existed next to the great river. They couldn't see the other side, but they knew they were finally on their last leg of the journey. They arrived in the town to find the residence friendly and eager for news of the west. Jo-Eb arranged for his small band of add-ons to take up residence there, and they immediately found themselves welcome. They were incorporated into a larger group who had managed to advance to this community as a separate entity, and since they were of the same clan, it meant the new group would be acclimated as members of the society.

16

Jo-Eb was anxious to continue on, so early the next morning, he and his explorer group headed for the banks to see if they could arrange for transport across the waters. He found that nobody wanted to cross, as there had been many rains to the north, and the locals were fearful that if they crossed, they would not be able to get back before the crest of the flood. When he made inquiries, he determined that the flood wasn't expected for several days and was informed that he could make the other side before it came. Determined not to get caught on this side of the river if he could avoid it he decided to purchase a worthy craft that would accommodate his crew, and he could continue. All except one were worthy seamen, and since all they had to do is cross a ten-mile stretch, he figured that it wouldn't pose a problem. After all, on his initial trip, he had purchased a rowboat and crossed it all by himself. After a bit of bargaining, they came up with a mutual price, and

Jo-Eb agreed to leave the boat on the far side with a banner attached, stating it belonged to the original owner. After all, he concluded, it would not be needed once the crossing was completed. Later, he reflected on that and concluded that we all make mistakes and that was one he wished he hadn't made. Nonetheless, the bargain was struck, and he paid the price.

Since they were a small party, they didn't have many belongings, and it didn't take long to set sail. It started out pleasant enough, but very quickly, they realized that things weren't as planned. Once they were in the main current, it started swiftly, moving them downstream. It didn't look that way from the shore, but like it or not, they were in for a ride. They pulled at the oars, attempting to direct themselves toward the other shore, and for a while, it seemed that despite the troubles they would soon be able to land on the far shore. At least, after the first couple of hours, they could see the land on the other side. With renewed hope, they redoubled their efforts, and it seemed that the worse was over. Just about that time, as often happens in life, they found that the push downstream was stronger, and despite their best efforts, they were being drawn back toward the center. Once again, they placed the extra oars in the water, and with four working in unison, it seemed that they were, in fact, going to make it. At that point, they heard the rumbling of the falls. The people at the boat docks told them about the falls but were confident that they would make the other side far above the area where that took place. Now what they knew was that the assumption was wrong. They were rapidly approaching the falls. Again, they redoubled their efforts to obtain the shore. One of the crew took a long rope with a makeshift anchor and threw it toward the shore as far as he could. It seemed to work, as their progress toward the falls slowed considerably. With that success, they rigged another anchor and again threw it as far toward the shore as they could muster. Once it indicated that it was secured, they pulled the boat as close to the original anchor and, with some difficulty, managed to dislodge it from its mooring. They had managed to keep the line on the second anchor, pulled tight, and were able to reign themselves closer to the bank. They repeated this several times, and it seemed to work except that each time they threw the new anchor out, they were drawn closer to the falls. The only question was if they would be able to successfully reach the calm waters before they came in contact with the raging falls. What they found was that as they got closer to the bank and the falls, they encountered rocks jutting above the surface, and they were able to lodge themselves between them to stem the force of the raging river. After several hours, they finally reached the other side and were in calm waters.

Exhausted, they pulled themselves up on the far bank and stopped to give thanks to God that all had eventually worked out. Barbara commented that it was appropriate to give thanks, as it was actually the first Thanksgiving day of the year. That was lost on some of those in the party, as they had never heard of a first and second Thanksgiving day. She explained that sometime in the far-flung past, a day had been set to give thanksgiving to God for His blessings. It had been lost for a few millenniums, and when it was rediscovered, they couldn't agree on the date of the original, so in deference to the wishes of both sides, two thanksgivings were established. After all, they thought you can't give thanks enough. They set up the camp and dispatched their guard force in the usual manner. With that accomplished, they decided that they had enough excitement for one day and would put off further travel until the next morning.

Soon they found themselves in the water again. The flood continued to rise, and they were almost swept down in a turret of raging water. They grabbed what they could and headed for higher ground. It seemed that no matter how high they climbed, the river was right on their heels. Despite the fact that they were plumb exhausted, they had to continue to climb or be swept away. That wasn't an option, as they would soon be pushed over the falls, and they were convinced that it would be the end of it all. At one point, Jo-Eb looked toward the sky and asked, "Lord, please help." He heard a voice in his mind, saying, *You have not because you ask not*. And the waters began to recede. The rest of the climb was uneventful, and when they reached the crest, they, for a second time, stopped and gave thanks.

After a good night's rest, they gathered up what was left of their belongings that hadn't gone over the side and set course for home. They traveled for several days and managed to secure some venison and, through the generosity of the people, were able to replenish much of what they had lost. The territory became a long line of simple rolling hills, and Jo-Eb could feel the excitement in his being. On the morning of the fourteenth day they topped the hill, he recognized a vaguely familiar site, and voila, they were home at last. They descended on the community with shouts of joy and expectations of friendly greetings. It didn't take long for him to be recognized, and he and his party were accepted as long-lost relatives even though the rest of them weren't actually relatives. "Any friend of Jo-Eb's is a friend of mine." The expression was continuously repeated. The word went out, and after only a short two hours, he found himself back in the arms of his wife and family. They had arrived about six months ago and identified themselves. Of course, they had been accepted into the family and were actually living in his aunt's old house.

A short time later, he was introduced to a lady that he had been seeking for some time now. Flower had returned to her home some four years ago and had married and now had three of her own. After the celebrations concluded and things calmed down, he made sure that all members of his party had been taken care of, then he accompanied Olivia and the kids back home.

He sat with his youngest on his lap. *The more things change,* he mused, *the more they remain the same.*